my Love never faked...

Trust me I still love you!

I0666537

my Love never faked...
Trust me I still love you!

Nikhil Mahajan

Srishti
PUBLISHERS & DISTRIBUTORS

SRISHTI PUBLISHERS & DISTRIBUTORS
N-16, C. R. Park
New Delhi 110 019
srishtipublishers@gmail.com

First published by Srishti Publishers & Distributors in 2010
Copyright © Nikhil Mahajan, 2010

Typeset in AGaramond 12pt. by Suresh Kumar Sharma at Srishti

To God, for his almighty support …

Acknowledgements

I would like to thank my "Bade Papa" who always saw a good writer in me, who always believed in my dreams and in my thoughts which further helped me to get on this platform other wise I would not have believed in myself.

I would like to thank my sweet lil' gf who gave me feelings with her luv when she entered my life, helped with the love story with the good times spent together and then finally by her silent breakup with the sad reasons which further gave me courage to speak out in the world, look into eyes of critics and face rejections. I would like to say her "sorry" too that I could not make up to her but the promises I had made will never be broken up and will be kept like a true gentle man..

"To answer her last words saying "don't hope" I would like to say that why I should not hope when I believe in myself and I trust on him."

Thanks to my room mate "Aman" who traveled with me all the way carrying my manuscript from one publication house to other and to support me when I broke up getting rejections from all sides...

I would like to thank my editor for giving a chance to a nascent writer and to believe in me that my emotions should be heard...

Thanks to all who discouraged me with their words, all the way strengthening me and my thoughts to go with my book further...

1
The start

The story starts with three friends on a bad day. It was a good noon, which was going to turn into a bad one. I was at my friend's college. Me, Ashit and Vicky, all were enjoying there, playing our usual funny mischievous games.

My name is Abhay, a Physiotherapy final year student. Jolly by nature and always looking for some mischief.

As we all know life without fun is like a well without water. So fun was our main motto whenever we visit each other's college.

Well! I like to be called Abhi, I have been given this name by my girlfriend, and her name is Priya. Priya and I were together from past 2 years and were enjoying our relationship together well.

I and Vicky decided to play this game. We had this college dictionary, we mean by library card book which has everyone's phone numbers entered to it... We pals use to call it college dictionary, where one can get all the bio data of the girls we admire.

So we went to college library and mostly boys like us always have an easy access to such things. We looked into it for details and there we have this one special number which was a mobile number rather than a land line.

Her name was Sana. We asked Ashit and enquired about this girl. Ashit showed us the girl and we had a good look at her. She was pretty as we expected by her name. So finally we decided to call her, we took her number and went upstairs at balcony from where we could easily have a good glance of the girl's room and where this girl was sitting. From here we could easily notice what she was doing.

I took my mobile and called her up.

"Hello!" in some enquiring manner I asked the girl while watching her from the balcony.

My heart started beating fast now. But in a second I regained confidence.

"May I know to whom I am speaking?" I asked politely in a soft voice.

As we all know first impression is the last impression.

"I'm Sana", she replied.

Now it was confirmed that the number belonged to this girl only to whom we were searching for, I continued the talk.

I said "If you don't mind and if I am not disturbing you, can I talk to you for a while?"

"Sure!" Sana replied back, not knowing our cunning intensions.

"But first tell me who are you?' she continued with a pause.

"You don't know me I am from this college only and I've been looking at you from past few months, I am your well wisher ", I said all in one breath as I was afraid that she might put down the line thinking that it must be some crazy guy calling her.

"What can I do for you?' said Sana.

"I wish to be your friend?" I replied in a straight manner.

Now it was Sana who has to reply me for my proposal, I crossed my fingers thinking it may be Heaven or may be a Hell now.

To my surprise she didn't says anything back and put off the call.

Now **it was a Do or Die situation** for me.

So I dialed her again.

"Why do you want to do friendship with me?" said Sana without listening me.

I didn't expect such good words from her but now it was bit assured that **Daal to gal rahi hai.**

While I was talking to her, Vicky and Ashit kept watching me.

Their eyes were confusing me even more and I was feeling shy, I wanted to be a stud in front of them so I concentrated more on talking.

"You got a lucky chance and you are asking me why?" I said to Sana, like a lottery master.

"I'm not interested and I haven't seen you, how can you think I'll say yes to you, this is very lame" replied the girl.

Now it was my turn to show my Ace card.

With confidence I said," If you will meet me, I am definitely sure that you can't say **no** to me".

"Come in front of me then we'll decide', said Sana.

And the call ends. It was now Vicky's turn and his part to play the game further.

The lover boy was all prepared for the moves. He took his Helmet, wore it and stood in the balcony.

I rang Sana again; called her to see if she was interested to meet me off if she was; then she could come to the balcony. I knew she won't come upstairs just to see this mysterious guy. So she tried to have a glance from the girl's room only. But she could not find any guy from the room.

She called me up this time.

"Hello, where the hell are you?" said Sana in an angry manner.

"Can't you see me I'm at balcony wearing a black shirt"; I reply back.

"Who?" asked Sana?

"The guy wearing a helmet?" she continued in an annoying way.

"Yes it's me dear?" I replied back.

"Why are you wearing this helmet and hiding yourself", says Sana.

"I feel shy, that's why?" I reply.

"C'mon you Jerk, Moron?" said Sana in a very pissed-off manner.

"Please say yes to me, and then I'll have confidence to remove this helmet, I feel shy like a new bride", I said.

"Then you should remain like this only ok and don't try to call me ever, I'll call police, blah blah"; said Sana.

Who was interested to hear all those words...

I could hardly hear any of her words as I was busy laughing at her so badly.

We had this all episode recorded in my mobile and it was a good prank for us to share. So with this incident we all came back home laughing.

At evening I got a call from Priya. She sounded very angry.

She just yelled at me and enquired where I was today.

I reply her softly. "At my friend's college"

Then she asked; "what happened there?"

I said 'Nothing happened much"

Hiding what happened at college, I was bit worried but then I thought how she could ever know about all the pranks we played there.

But one should know that girls have a good network and you can't really hide anything from them...

"Who is Sana?" Priya said with anger.

'Who" I said with fear in my mind, I knew I was caught and some blunder is going to happen.

I had already recognized the prank girl but I didn't want to show her.

"You proposed her?" said Priya.

"No I didn't"; I reply.

To escape the argument; I uttered softly "Vicky did".

"And it was a prank'; I continued further.

"You are lying!" said Priya.

I asked "who told you".

"That's none of your business but who so ever told me, I believe that person" said Priya.

"How can you believe some outsider?" I tried to shield myself now.

I thought it would be golden words but Priya's words shook me up "I saw your number on her mobile and she also told me the whole episode this noon only!"

A thought came into my mind (**kisi ne sach kaha tha ki kahyi peyi nahi aur glass toda 2 lakh ka**).

But it was of no use then. Priya was not going to listen to me, I knew her nature.

I acted smartly.

"Sorry baby, it was a mere joke we did in the college"; I acted like confessing.

"It was a bet'; I continued.

"Hmm"; Priya could say this only now.

I could hear her voice like she had tears in her eyes.

"I am a loser and I came to know you are the only girl who can love this boy so much"; I **started lagao makkhan** now.

Some wise words, you can't win from a girl and if you start winning over her, she would cry and you have to admit your fault. So the crux is what ever you do, you are a looser!

"I did it and I am sorry for whatever happened today, now I'll not do anything like this again and will never go to my friend's college again"; I spoke like promising her.

"I believe you" Priya replied like she was satisfied from my confession.

I could hardly believe myself how this episode ended up so early with out any fight. May be insecurity to loose someone dearer is the dirtiest feeling in the world.

A nightmare that no one wants to have in his/ her life time. But my skin was safe now and so I was happy.

I further talked to her in a nice way and then we didn't discuss this thing further. I rang up Ashit after her call, tell him the whole episode and told him that I am not going to enter his college again as now, as I have promised Priya and would like to be loyal with her always.

He kept laughing at me and on the whole episode.

2

All men are dogs

As we all know **men are dogs**, lol!

So am I.

Vicky called me up in the morning very next day after the Sana's episode took place.

"We are going to college, I have practical's to attend"; Vicky said.

"Okay I'll be on time at our **adda**" I replied; without thinking about my promise to Priya

Adda – a place common in all our friends to meet, where we discuss about girls and cricket most of time...

I was excited to visit his college so my promise to Priya was secondary to me at that time.

By the time I left for **adda** on my scooter. Vicky was already waiting for me. Ashit also came just while before me on his bike. We kicked our rides and in 5 minutes we reached at the gate of the College.

I had this feeling of fear in my heart now that I was doing was wrong. But who doesn't want to peek at girls…?

Every guy wants to see girls so my fear ended in a moment and I was in the College. With one step into the college, I was in and the fear was out.

I was in Heaven again, girls every where. I mean guys were there but **un salon ko kaun dekhta hai**.

I went to ground to play Volley ball. Vicky went to attend the class and Ashit gave me company.

The sun was over head and we were losing. Bad day I guess, as we had never lost and we had money on the game.

RINGING

I felt like my mobile ring. My heart pounded, Priya must be calling to check, I thought. I took my mobile and looked at the screen. The number was unknown to me. Priya must be checking from some friend's mobile or may be some one else but I had to pick up the call.

"Hello!" I said.

"Hello "; a manly voice which I could hardly recognize.

I felt voice is recognizable but could not able to make it. But the voice was sad

"Is this Abhi on the other side of the call?", said the caller. I had fishy thoughts in my mind.

"Who are you?" I said in a bossy manner. I didn't want this guy to know me.

"It's me, Manav"; said the caller.

I dug my mind as the name was sound familiar.

"Manav is that you? Dog!!, from where are you calling today?" I reply in a happy mood.

Manav was my college mate and was a very good friend of mine. We were studying together from past 2 years and I wonder why I could not recognize his name. He didn't had any mobile and this number of mine, may be that's why.

"Where are you and what are you doing?" I said.

"Result is out?"; Manav told me with out any other talks.

"Congrats!"; I said.

"This is serious Abhi, your result isn't good"; said Manav.

"You have failed in one subject", continue Manav.

I felt like a volcano had just burst out somewhere coz I haven't expected it to happen and none of my exam went bad. I was good at studies also, then how could this happen to me!

"Call you later"; said Manav and he put down the line.

I could only hear beep-ring in my phone, but nothing was pleasant now. The Angels around me seemed like devil. I felt like all girls are staring at me as if they know my result. I felt insulted, I decided to leave before I collapsed.

"I'm going"; I said to Ashit.

'We have one set pending"; said Ashit back.

"I have to leave, I have an urgent work at home"; I replied while I took small steps and came out of ground.

"Are you ok?" asked Ashit

'You never leave the game?", Ashit continued following me.

"I have to go", I said and in no time I was out.

In my heart's heart I had this feeling; there must be some mistake at university level. May be Manav is playing a prank on me this can't happen to me." Let's wait till evening and all will be fine till then", I said to myself.

Prank will be over by then or may be some of my classmate will call me with congrats, SMS wishing me that I had passed. But the truth is truth and I had to face it. With the thoughts in my mind and a broken heart I moved towards the gate of the College. I reached near my scooter; kicked it without looking at it. By that time I started thinking; how to tell this bad news at home? I was feeling ashamed of myself as I can't even lie to them because it was my last year and I had to collect my documents from university. I started moving out of the college with many thoughts and ideas in my mind. Thinking about what could be done? How to tell mom and dad about my result?

If I would going to hide, sooner or later they would come to know of it from my friends or someone else.

I raced my scooter and in a minute I was on road heading towards home with the bad news. These things kept moving in my mind so badly, that I was nearly struggling to drive. Just 3 minutes on the road and I'll be at my home. But the time seemed to be running slower and slower. About a km ride or so, I felt that sun is going to blow me up. I felt cold and all in sweat, my head started aching.

I didn't know what was happening to me but it seemed like my thoughts had taken over my consciousness level. I felt partially unconscious then, or may be I was in a sub conscious level. I could hear the sound of the buses louder than the actual audible level, in a sec when I shook my head and I found that I was in wrong side of the road.

I was driving on the right side and an army truck was heading towards me.

In a second, like a wise driver I took control of the my scooter and I changed my lane. Without looking back and being unaware of this fast bike coming from behind I crashed with him. He with his speed, dashed into the chassis of my scooter and finally I was lying on the road looking at the sky. I could hardly remember what else happened to me.

When I opened my eyes, I found myself at home. My friends surrounded me, mom was crying and dad was looked at me as if the whole mistake was mine. At this time I could not think about my result coz the situation was tense.

Relatives started visiting me talking about how and when it happened.

I had to repeat the story so many times to them, that I started getting irritated by it.

I had a broken rib and a hair line fracture on foot. Pain was unbearable, but not more than I had in my mind of the result. The thought came into my mind at was the right time to tell mom and dad about the truth because am on bed and no body is going to yell at me at this hard time. I uttered everything to them on which they responded very gently. I was enjoying sympathy from their part now.

This world is so beautiful when you have a bad result and yet you are enjoying in bed. Get up late in the morning, brushing your teeth at noon, after the brunch. Two days passed with all these kind of stuff (**aur ab to maaza bhi aane laga tha**) but now I was getting bored of this home kind of sick life. I needed some fun on daily basis but because of my broken foot I didn't have permission to go out; moreover the scooter was at workshop for repair.

———**Days passed**———

One day at noon about twelve o'clock I was alone at home, suddenly bell rings.

Ding...

I looked around; no one was expected at this time. I answered the door.

"Hello sir" said a man with a moustache standing at my door.

He looked like a sale's man to me.

"Hello", I replied.

"Where is your phone? Is it working properly?" enquired the man.

"Yes there it is" I pointed towards the table, while I replied. Showing him the phone I let him enter the house.

He was carrying a box in his hand. He handed me a box and asked me to sign the delivery papers. I read it carefully and then I came to know, what was the broadband connection, I had applied for, a month ago.

The box was my gift- a modem.

I had a smile on my face, and I was so happy to know it that I even forgot to offer the man a glass of water. May be he wasn't so thirsty, so he gave me the catalogue and went out. And no time I tore the box and plugged the equipment as per the manual, the wires were provided. Everything went fine.

I followed the procedure whatever written in the manual and then attached the modem to my computer and from one side to the phone outlet. With some installations and a click of a button I connected my computer to the internet. It was my lifeline from now.

My wish had come true after such a bad phase. I was ready to have some fun. But before that, I needed some good computer softwares. I installed the messenger and some other applications needed for fun. That day I switched off my mobile for the whole day to enjoy with no disturbance.

Priya kept calling me but who cared now for her. I was so then addicted to Internet, I checked my e-mail. Did some messenger stuff.

And kept myself busy whole day.

Next day was Saturday and I knew my friends were going to visit me. I had no escape from it so I decided to tell them myself about the internet connection otherwise they will make it an issue.

I called Vicky up and told him about the broadband connection. He sounded happier than me and was excited too. The days were passing peacefully with my broadband now. At night, I called Priya to patch-up, said sorry to her and made a story that my mobile's battery was low and that's why I could not call her up...

Next morning, I wake up late because I had this chit bit with Priya late last night. It was 11 o'clock by my watch, the sun was on head. I opened my curtains, did my regular morning activities.

Phone rang.

"Hello Abhi we are coming to your house, we have bunked our classes"; murmured Vicky.

Before I could make any silly excuse, the phone got disconnected. I knew now Vicky will be here any minute.

Bell rang again, this time it was door bell.

I opened the door. To my surprise it was Ashit.

"Hi dude! how are are?" entered Ashit.

"Well fine" I replied to him.

"I just heard this morning you've got broadband connection dude?" enquired Ashit, while entering the house.

Vicky had already told Ashit that I had got my broadband connection. And they were here to do crazy work on internet now. Ashit was in and I offered him some juice.

Bell rang again.

'*Darwaza khol*' it was Vicky's voice.

I opened the door; pushing me aside Vicky entered with a big smile on his face with snacks and drinks in his hand.

"Switch it on man" said Vicky while sitting on computer table chair.

I pointed toward the button and asked Ashit to switch it."

Ashit bent over and switched it on and then I connected it to the internet. Vicky was in some **masti mood**. I was unaware of his intensions. He was much into computers and knew much about internet too.

"Speed is cool!" Vicky giggled in excitement.

"What are you going to do? and why did you call me?" asked Ashit.

"I have my class" he continued.

"Going to show you some thing baby!" clinked Vicky.

I was still confused and was unaware of Vicky's next step.

"What are you gonna do ?" I said in a harsh tone because if he would do something wrong, I would be held responsible at home.

"I want to know what's on your mind." I asked him, time going closer to the table.

Vicky said in excitement "Have you ever heard about some escort websites on internet?"

"That's what we are going to try" continued Vicky.

On my part, I was excited too, hearing Vicky's idea about watching porn.

Trying to be a responsible guy, I didn't show him any expression on my face but I was into this game back then.

"I do have some names of such websites" said Vicky boldly.

In a click he entered a name, and in a flash we were surprised to see the scene on the screen. We could see every kind of girl - Indians, Russians, Latin, Americans.

Wow! It was exciting! who cares about girls now?, a though feel my mind. I was also smiling. Our eyes were wide open looking at the screen with full concentration. I might not had shown such an interest even about my studies like I keen that moment here. Within 5 minutes a message popped up screen.

Get a user name and password.

All the excitement had sucked, as we glanced message. As we headed down to the page, we had sad faces looking at the form, asking for credit card payments. We closed the website and started searchy for another one. There was hardly any free website which could provide us some stuff.

"Fuck those who made these websites!" said Vicky.

"I thought we would look at every page of the site but it seems they need money from us" added Ashit to his statement.

"No fun" I said, nodded my head like it didn't matter much to me.

All the fun was gone.

But as we all know (**khali dimaag shaitan ka ghar.**)

"I have a solution" whispered Ashit.

"What is the solution" Vicky asked Ashit.

"My dad's credit card" Ashit said, with a wicked smile on his face.

"Will it do? I can help you if it's for three dollars only and not more than that" said Ashit.

Those three dollars were like door to heaven to us

With no time I said "Ok, tell us c.c number and pin number"?

"I don't have it now but I'll bring it and would look for the files for the code" said Ashit.

"Go get it" I ordered Ashit.

I was clear from my voice that now I was more excited too now. Ashit was now feeling sorry that he uttered that his dad owns a credit card. But since he told us he has to get it and he knew it.

Ashit took his bike and went home to get the card and code.

Till then we listened to some rock and chilled ourselves.

Vicky connected to some internet radio stations and helped me with some software solutions. After an hour or so Ashit came back with his dad's credit card number and the 'code'.

("*lo salon tumhare liye kya kya karna padta hai?*") said Ashit like he had just climbed mount Everest.

But the consequences were same, we knew that if we got caught we are gonna to be thrown out of our houses. But excitement was more than the punishment. This time we opened some web with camming kind of stuff.

"These websites provides cam to cam chatting"; said Vicky.

I and Ashit kept looking at the screen. We could see a moving girl but faded coz we were still not registered to the website. Vicky filled a form and some details.

"Done, we have our user name and password"; said Vicky proudly.

"What's the user name and password?" I enquired.

I wanted to know because I was thinking it would be better if we all knew it, as money matters, especially from Ashit's dad wallet.

"Purpledog" said Vicky.

"What's this?" Ashit asked.

"This is our username to view some good girls" said Vicky with a smile.

"Password" I asked this time.

"Angelview" replied Vicky.

"Let's start it now" said Ashit.

And with one click we were into the chat room with one girl at side and every kind of dogs barking at her at other side. Some were so impolite to her that we could not even imagine...

"Let's type something" I said to Vicky as he was near the keyboard.

Vicky's hand moved towards the keyboard.

"What to write' asked Vicky.

This time it was Ashit's head. He always rescuded us when it comes to us if brains. I was busy looking at this girl. She was in lingerie and was typing something. I could see our user name with Hello on the screen.

"Bitch write us something" I said to Ashit.

"Lets us also reply to her" said Ashit.

"Hello" typed Vicky in no time.

I was surprised how he could write so fast on the board and then I thought I might also have written if I was so close to the screen.

"How are you?" reply came on the screen.

I was bit confused coz we were new to the website.

"Does she know us?" it was Ashit with his usual poor joke.

"Nah this is her duty and this is for what she is paid" said Vicky trying to explain. He was feeling proud I could see Vicky had a smile on his face.

It was awesome and I did some mischief after so long.

I was on cloud nine. My life ends in a day if I don't do something crazy.

"I am ok" typed Vicky.

"Where are you from?" Vicky typed again.

I was still looking at her on the screen and was uninterested to see what Vicky and Ashit were typing. The scene was so wonderful and the girl was beautiful like   F-TV model.

She was half nude in front of us. People were asked dirty questions about her sizes and she smiled and replied smart peaky. We were excited in short. But the excitement couldn't take us so far until we mixed up with other people in chat room and asked her some dirty questions of our likings too.

'What are your sizes?"

"Are you a virgin?"

"What you will like to show?"

"You are a naughty bitch!!"

All kind of questions that we could ever ask a girl, we asked her. We asked everything her as if we owned her for three dollars.

Oh! Gosh such a lovely sigh it was, looking at her.

She did her some special moves while she typed. Seemed like some one else was typing for her, but who cared. We were here to watch her till our account lasts.

We watched her for about 3 hours and time went so fast, I could not imagine.

"Let's go now" said Ashit.

"5 min more" replied Vicky.

And 5 minutes ended up quickly I was still wondering how time could pass so quick so early today with internet.

3

Date with my angel

I wrote the username and password on my computer table. I had the idea to see the cam at night alone. I took my lunch, as it was already late. It was 6 in the evening now, mom and dad, all were at home. I lied down on the bed as if I was still not fine. By this time I had forgotten everything about the result. I had other things in my mind those were rather more exciting.

I called Priya. It was necessary too because I hadn't called her up for some time and I was sure she would be angry with me so I rang her up and we had great talks about our life. We decided to give time to each other and make a good plan for the very evening.

Priya was upset with me but since I know her likings well I gave her time to meet me at ice cream parlor. She got convinced.

I took **auto rickshaw** to the near by Ice-cream shop. I Waited for her and knew it well she would be late as always. After about 15 minutes or so, Priya entered Ice cream parlor. She was looked like an angel as always, wearing a white top. I always use to say she looks like an angel when she wears white may be that's why she has mostly white dresses only. I looked at her hand; she was holding something in it. She had a card with her.

Looking at card I assured myself, again I had completely forgotten the special day. Yes it was the special day, it was 2nd. Me and Priya always use to celebrate 2nd of every month because on 2nd October may be November I proposed her few years ago. And we still fought about, whether it was October or November but neither of us remembered the exact month. Reaching near the table where I was sitting Priya came with a big smile forgetting all fights.

"For you sweetie" said Priya, handing me the card.

I got the indications that she might be expecting at least a card from me in return. I opened the card and read it:

"To the person who sweetens my life with his presence"

This was the quotation written in it. I felt very sorry because I hd forgot it again and it was something I kept every month continuously.

Looking at my face me knew it that I had forgotten it again and the good ice-cream date turned out into melted ice cream night mare. We had ice creams but on different table. I took my card with myself and got home. Like always on the way, I bought a good card for her.

For Priya it was always 3rd of month, the special day because I hardly remembered if I ever give her card on the very day she gave.

"To a girl as favorite as my favorite ice cream "

This was my quotation I had in my mind for her because we had just met on ice-cream parlor.

I wrote it on the card and I gave it to Priya and the fight finally ended, I promised never to forget the 'special day'.

——*8ᵗʰ May*——

Last year, Sunday, the day was fine. It was my pre-examination time. I was at my rented room playing on my laptop. Listening some good music and playing videogames with my friends. Life was just chilling and my room was like a club.

Panni and Manav were at my house for some guess work but no one was interested to study. Varun the third friend, was out to watch a movie with his girlfriend. We were all by the preparatory holidays.

I was unaware of the bigger trouble on my way while enjoying the game. We had money on it, so wining was necessity too. Manav had ashtray in his hand and was making puffs of his lighted cigarette.

"My turn!" said Manav.

I turned the laptop to his side.

Bang bang slash the car dig into the wall...

Lol, it was Manav's turn and he was playing bad in his turn. So by points Panni was winning the game.

"Party from my side ' said Panni.

"Beers on me" he continued.

I was happy on my part at least I deserve one beer.

Beep

My cell was full of received messages and I was uninterested to read any of them.

Free messages from friend, clicked my mind. I didn't bother to open them at all.

Varun entered the room with a movie in his hand; I took the CD case and looked at the cover for details.

Panni was still busy with the game and Manav was making puffs out of his cigarette. Varun looked at my mobile.

"You have 7 messages Abhi" Varun told me looking at the screen.

"Some kind of advertisements" I replied showing no care.

Varun opened the messages while I kept looking at the star cast on the CD cover.

I was excited to watch the movie. Sunday and movie, all college students want this.

"It's from Priya"; said Varun.

"5 from Priya's number and 2 from unknown numbers" Varun said again lifting the cell and waving it towards me.

I shook my head, and took a deep breath I could smell some kinda fight now. What could she do to me "I'll ask sorry to her and everything would be fine" I said to myself.

"Baby you didn't call me up yet, do you remember anything? luv ya"

I read the message in my mind. Taking this not much seriously I opened the second message

"I kept waitn all night for your wishes, at least you could messaged me a b'day wish!

I think you have forgotten it!!"

I felt like crying dat time. The matter was serious.

"Today is Priya's b'day and I didn't wish her." I said it a bit louder.

Varun, Panni and Manav stared at me.

"Then what, Call her up and wish her" said Manav cigarette still lightened up and taking a deep puff. I wonder how many cigarettes he took?, while I was busy with everything.

'Ya man, call her up tell her you took sleeping pills at night or you were busy studying hard for examination at night" said Panni looking at computer screen with his ever usual lame excuses.

Nothing was helping me, as we all knew.

kuch bhi karlo saala ladkion k liye kamm par he jaate hai

I knew Priya was expecting my call at very 12 o'clock. I was a fool.

"I could have put an alarm to the day on my cell"; I said worryingly.

I searched the phone saved numbers, looked for her name and

called her up but the phone was switched off. Nothing could be done now. Only some tsunami or an earthquake could help me out now and nothing is going to happen. To help me only God has to appear on earth and he'll save me.

I kept on trying her number while thinking all this bullshit...

Thinking of her and her how angry would she. I was afraid of to call her now.

I opened the main menu of the phone.

3 more messages

My mobile was still beeping.

I checked other messages; two were **shayari** messages from some numbers…

Then I open the 3 rd message..

"**ab tum mujhe fir se wish karna bhul gaye**"

<You forgot to wish me again>

I kept thinking in my mind what else I am forgot.

May be today is her mom's b'day. No.

May be today is her dad's b'day. No.

Then what today is her grandfather's b'day. No.

What the hell I was forgetting…….??

I pressed down the message the message was incomplete yet.

"You didn't wish me, today is my examination!!"

I remember at once, that Priya keep telling me, that she was preparing for M.A.T. examination but I had kept on ignoring it and today was the date for examination.

"What time is it?' I asked my friends.

"12: 30' answered Panni.

He was still busy with laptop and the game. He had his own things to do which are more important than my problems. Well the problem was mine so, it was me who had to solve it.

"Ah' came from my mouth.

"She will be in the examination hall" I said loudly.

'Who?" asked Manav his cigarette dangling from his mouth.

"Priya, I still have a chance if I'll be there for her, I can" I said hopefully.

"What?" said Varun still confused.

"Nothing I want to be there outside her examination hall"; I said.

"Lemme get ready" I continued.

In no time I went to bathroom to freshen up. Get ready with out any comb, gel up my hair. Wear shirt which ever came first within my reach.

"Take me to examination center" I begged Varun.

Varun had his bike parked outside the house and I knew he drives really fast. He was the only guy who could help me out now. In 2 minutes we were at the parking. Varun kicked the bike and I got onto the backseat.

"Get me to a card shop first", I asked Varun.

"Ok boss" Varun acted like a robot. He could feel my tension and excitement.

"As fast as you could" I said.

Varun drove as fast he could. I could feel air in my ears and mouth too. It felt like I was on mission Mars this time. Trucks were not giving us pass, but doing some wrong drive and action we reached at card gallery. I took one card, the b'day one. Borrowed a pen from the gallery keeper, and wrote:

"Happy b'day "and "luv u always"

I could hardly remember any quotation and I didn't need any in such a situation.

"Where to go?" asked Varun.

"Oh my God I didn't even ask her for the examination center!!" I said with my hand on my face.

"Are you nuts you don't even know her examination center!!" Varun was surprised by my words and he knew the situation was now going out of control.

Nothing seemed to come into my mind now to save myself.

I forgot her b'day. Didn't wish her good luck and now I don't even know her center for examination? It was too bad on my part. Only thing I could do was to go out all the examination centers in the town but this was not such a good idea.

As we all know when nothing comes to your mind and you're in trouble, just close your eyes concentrate on the trouble, there you'll get the hidden solution. I closed my eyes and I tried to remember Priya's talk, she might have told me something about her center which I kept skipping in my mind. There was nothing such a hidden solution. It was because of my deeds I was suffering.

Then I tried to remember who else was preparing for MAT examination. There was my solution. It was Vicky from my friend circle was also preparing for the same exam and I knew he might have talked to Priya about her examination center.

I took my mobile searched for Vicky's number. Called him up.

"Hello"

"Vicky **bhai** where are you?" I asked without going into any other details.

"It's me Ashit" I got reply from other side.

"Vicky is in examination hall you can call him later" continued Ashit.

"**Bhai** I need help, you know, where's Priya's examination center?" I questioned Ashit.

"How can I know your Gf's examination center, I hardly talk to her" Ashit reply back.

It seemed like he was laughing at me. I had no choice other than putting the line off.

Taking some risk won't kill you. So I decided to leave no stone unturned.

But I needed to be rescued. I decided to call Priya's home. I called her up at her home phone number.

"Hello who is this calling?" seemed like Priya's mother was at other end.

She knew about me but we never talked much as we had some bad conversations before, when I used to roam near Priya's house her mother got the impression that I am a big **loafer**.

"Namaste aunty ji" I said respectfully.

"Hanji beta, who is this??" replied Priya's mom.

I could easily understand that she might have recognized my voice and is going to blow me now.

"It's me Vicky" I lied in a low pitch.

"Yes Vicky beta, how are you?" asked Priya's mom.

"Fine aunty ji", I said.

"Where's Priya and why is her mobile switched off" I continued the conversation and indirectly came to my point.

"She's gone for examination that's why her mobile is switched off", answered Priya's mom to my silly question.

I was scared of getting so I went straight to the point now.

'Which place?" I asked.

"University", Priya's mom replied.

That was all I needed from hear.

"Bye aunty ji will call you later", I uttered while disconnecting the call.

I put off the line and in no time I asked Varun again. "Let's move to university".

Before I could complete my sentence, Varun was ready to go as he already had listened university from my mouth, while I was talking with Priya's mother.

The day was bad and was getting worse with each passing moment. Each time we reached the traffic light the signal turned red and this started wasting our time. It was bad timing and bad luck.

"Fuck! red light again"; yelled Varun looking at light.

Numbers were being displayed on it showing us how much to wait and this was like killing time in a bad situation where each second was costing my life. It was a 30 second wait but I could not wait for even a second. Time slipping away and the bike wasn't moving.

"*Isko bhi abhi hona tha!!*', I said to myself in pain as if someone dissecting me with a surgeon's scalpel.

"What you want me to do?" said Varun.

I said "cross the red light"

This was something Varun was waiting for to hear from me and wasting no time Varun raced the bike and crossed the traffic line, some action movie songs kept buzzing in my mind as we reached around the 90 speed.

It was the last light to cross and in about 5 minutes we entered the university campus in front of examination hall. I kept looking at rooms whether they were empty or examination was going on.

There was no one there; exam has just finished 15 min ago. It was tough one, one boy keep saying it. I got so sad that we could not make it after doing so much efforts.

"What to do now?" I ask Varun.

"Call her and ask her where she is?" Varun reply me.

I took my mobile and dialled her number. The phone was not off this time.

We could hear a ringing tone near us. I looked back near to a tree. There stood a girl with a mobile in her hand wearing a white kurta and blue jeans. I knew it was her, waiting for me as if she knew I will come over there.

I went close to her, and looked into her eyes. Varun remained there as if he was uninterested in our **pyar ki baatein.** Looking in eyes I felt my heart ache.

I was happy and felt like I had traveled across the whole world for my Angel. Yes she was looking like an angel. I broke the silence.

"I am sorry", I said fearfully.

"Happy b'day", I continued.

"Thank you "; reply Priya.

"How was your exam?" I put my second question and tried to change the topic.

"Good", she replied without looking at me.

She was looked sad by the time.

'How long have you been waiting for me?" I asked her handing over my card to her.

"15 minutes or so"; she answered me, while looking at envelope.

"But may be one day I'll not wait for u, I'll be gone Abhi before you will realize my importance"; said Priya.

"You won't be doing so" I replied with a smile.

"Yes I will do it, because you don't care for me", Priya said with a pain in her eyes and her voice was soft this time and I could see sparkling tear in her eyes shining like a pearl coz of shining sun.

"Isn't it?" Priya asked again, and her words hurt me because I was at fault and I admit it.

"I care for you Priya" this much I could answer to her.

"How you came to know about my examination hall"; Priya questioned me this time to lighten the serious mood.

"I called up your mom"; I replied to her question with a wicked smile on my face.

"She told u? You took such a risk?" Priya was surprised this time.

"Anything for you" I replied more mischievously.

"Are you nuts she will come to know because Vicky was also preparing for MAT??" 'Priya said horrified.

And the usual fight continued again. In our relation we only fight, fight and fight but one thing was for sure we loved each other so much that after every fight, we used to take blame on ourselves.

I never wanted to, but I guess I always give reasons to her.

This kept moving in my mind how come Priya's mother helped

me today, may be she knows that it's me Abhi calling. She knew my number and she knew my voice too. Who cares Priya was in my arms now, my angel and this world seems to be in my arms.

That evening Priya called me up. She said she liked my card where it was written **to my wife**, Man, I had given her a relation greeting and I had not noticed that.

But this card gave me more opportunity to impress her that how much I care for her and for our future...

Priya was happy looking at card. She said yes, she wants to marry me soon after she'll finish her MBA course.

Ladkio ko hum kaise samajh sakte hain jabhi upar waala bhi samajh nahi paaya.

This poem is so true because it tells what I felt about Priya.

My favorite melted ice-cream

My favorite melted ice-cream,
Was like in a steam,
It was melted it was tasteless,
But was my favorite,
So was not baseless...

I still respect it like a new,
It was something I eat a few,
I liked it hard with some cashew,
I like to lick it and to chew,
I don't afford to let it melt,
But there was something in my heart I did felt...

I always ate it on a good day,
But today nothing was good as it pay,
I was melted like my ice cream,

My girl had just made me scream,
She was angry so was I,
But not to fight I just try,

She just has to say something,

So I was left for nothing,

I tried to eat it all but cant,

Am I goanna leave it for a grant...

This ice cream I always shared with my girl,

But now it was melted shining like a pearl,

Sometime we had fight for a last bite,

I always give her yes it was right

Now neither my ice cream nor my girl was good,

I tried to make it favorite as I could........

Luv ya always

4

An ordinary day

I was at home, alone, it was Sunday. All my friends went to river to enjoy their weekend. I was one of the people who would make such plans, most of the Sunday mornings. I love to chill there but due to my plastered foot I had to stay at home.

Friends called me up in the morning, asking me as if I can join them but how could I? They knew it but have to ask me before going.

I lay in bed. I was feeling lonely. Mom and dad were out because dad's boss had a party and dad has to attend it at any cost.

I turned on the TV. Wow M-TV roadies, I like this show very much. Back bitching, Ragghu was scolding the participants. I enjoy it but it didn't lasted for long. Time runs so quickly when you start enjoying. Show had to end sooner or later I knew. I turned off the TV. It was hard time for me to spend time home alone. I came back to my room, turned on my computer looking for some interesting activity.

I opened my messenger so that I can chat with some friend's online and spend some time but there was no one to have fun. Then I looked at the chat list.

Yeah! Purpledog

It was glowing like a golden coin put on the table. I opened the porn website which Vicky used that day.

And put this user name and password.

Kept looking at screen I could see many girl's name who were online to chat with their porn picks on top of their names. There was a name with no pic and it was a pic saying new comer

Taking no time I decided to click on her name and to enter her chat room. It took a little longer than usual to approve at her room. Room was bit empty and there were hardly three users. The girl was looking pretty with clothes on.

She was a blond girl very beautiful with big hazel eyes. She was a bit healthy. Looking like a teenage girl.

"Take off your clothes"

"Bitch"

"C'mon give us some pleasure"

All such messages kept popping up on the screen. It was a usual sight for me till now.

She could hardly type anything in reply as if she was not used to it.

"Hi' I typed.

"Hi Purpledog" she answered from other side.

"How are you?" I typed again.

"Am fine" she replied.

"Where r u from?" I asked her.

I was being as polite as I could.

"Russia" she repled.

"Kool I am from India" I typed.

And we talked about many silly things for an hour.

I had noticed from far and Vicky already had told me that these girls on porn websites keep on changing their names so that one guy can't follow them again and again and harass them.

Thought came into my mind "I didn't want to lose this girl."

I could remember her user name but it was of no use.

Her id was xxxblondbabe.

But I had to be sure enough that I know more about her to catch her again if I wanted to chat with her.

I typed: "I like you very much and want to chat with you more but I have to go now."

"Please stay with me for a while" she typed back.

She seemed she was interested to chat with me like I was. This was something I wanted from her.

Well-well who doesn't want to be respected, I had respected this girl a lot so she was with me. With more respect now, I start saying, "Ma'am" to her. I knew it was still a chance but I kept chatting with her, asking.

"Miss blonde! What you like to eat and all this kind of stuff."

While other people keep on repeating:

"Come to me"

"Come on babe"

"Fuck and all"

I knew I had made an impression on her.

I said "I have to go, is there's any how I could catch you later?"

"No' she replied again.

I too was not in a mood to go but I was just checking her wish and I was trying to tease her.

She was alone so she wanted to spend some time with me.

"I want to give you my mobile number so that we can maintain contact if you wish to?" I typed straightaway now.

To my surprise no message came back from her side. It only came some dotted lines because the webmaster had locked it so that people don't share personal information to these girls.

"It didn't come"; I type.

"Ya I know" she types back.

"Anything I can do now"; I asks her.

"Nothing'; she answers.

But I had already decided, I would anything for it I knew. I said I'll give you my email id from there we can continue. I typed my messenger id. But nothing came again.

"Don't use @"; she typed back helping me this time.

"Ok' popped into the screen.

"Sugarboy" I typed giving her my messenger id.

"Am waitn for you at messenger for friend request."

"Ok after some time when my time will be over here" she repled.

I closed the website and logged on to my messenger. I started waiting for her there.

It came into my mind, why am doing all this for a stranger? Why I am waiting for her? I waited for an hour but no request came.

Ring!!

I looked at my phone. Priya was calling me. I had to leave now. I closed messenger and picked up the phone. Priya's voice was what I wanted to hear at this time. This was what I was missing the most.

I had totally forgotten about her these days as I was busy peeking into cams looking for some porn stuff. I repent on my deeds, what I was doing in my life, when it was so much ok and so smooth.

Priya was happy; I could easily notice this by hearing her "hello" to me on phone. I was bit confused how this can happen as I have ignored her for so many days and now she is not up to any fight. I talked with her properly as if I was not doing anything wrong by ignoring her.

"Abhi, u know why am I happy?"

Many thoughts came into my mind. May be Priya's mother had started, liking me. Priya's dad wants us to get us married. I could not think of anything else.

"Have I done something special for her?" the thought came to my mind and I kept thinking in my mind again and again.

"I have decided to go for a summer job; I have got a call from the office to join" Priya said in a merry way.

"Congrats" I wished her half heartedly.

I knew if she'll be in office I won't be able to talk to her. But from other half of my heart I was happy because now I will have a lot of time to spend, but with whom. Every boy wants to go on the road to gaze at girls. I could not go such coz every gal will give me a cold shoulder if Id be wearing plaster and rolling my eyes over them.

Friends were busy and now Priya was also busy. Loneliness was the best partner.

The thought fitted me well, we used to talk on phone but I knew now it will be impossible. I didn't want to meet her as I was sad about her decision. We shared some good thoughts, some love lines and time passed away.

Her parents came back home so she ended the conversation leaving me alone with a last love note.

"Okay bye Abhi luv ya take care of your self" said Priya in a very loving way.

"Ya bye, but tell me when are we going to talk again" I knew it was hard.

"I don't know" Priya said in a sad tone.

"Well soon" she said again trying to cheer me up.

"From tomorrow I am joining the office" she continued.

I kept silent. I could not say anything more I was in pain and tears.

"Bye luv you too, take care" I ended the conversation from my side.

I put off the line and lay on bed thinking what to do next.

Beeps

My mobile vibrates, it was a message.

I look at the message.

Message: "Hope you understand you didn't sound happy while talking but I had to have some experience before I join my course'

I got the answer, ah I was fool to think I was more important.

I typed a message for her:

"No probes' baby I can wait for you for the whole life time"

To be a little romantic I add up some pick up line.

"I one who would be there and would love you even when your hair turned white."

"You may not have teeth left."

"You could not see without glasses."

"But I'll be there for you, holding your hand."

I knew these words will definitely make her cry. But I was feeling that way.

I remained lying till mom and dad called me up for dinner. We had dinner together while watching TV after a long time. I was forced to watch news coz dad wanted to watch the daily headlines. And I knew after the news we are going to have some hard talks about what we watched, what is happening to the nation. I ate my dinner fast so that I could skip the extra news innings.

But dad had other things in mind. Today extra innings started soon. It was on the news "Young children use internet with intensions."

We watched news. Ya it was interesting till they were telling us some good porn website addresses and when they were talking about children being addicted to internet and killing themselves. Huh. How can these news channels make us believe that if someone at other side will tell us to kill, we would commit suicide but the shit has actually happened somewhere in the world.

We had our conversation over it. Dad keeps blaming internet for bad outcomes and I was defending myself because I was using internet and he knew it.

I kept saying these children are fools if they do such nuisance. And the conversation ended up when I stood from table and went to my room angrily. Now I was in no mood to turn on my computer and use internet. I lay on bed.

Beep

My mobile vibrates. I look at its screen. There were 3 messages and 5 missed calls.

I first looked at missed calls. Priya had called me up half an hour ago. I repented for missing it because it was a lucky chance as were never had such good luck when Priya could call me up at night time for a chit chat.

I overcame the trauma. Searched for messages.

I opened the 1st message

"pyar to dokha hai hai yeh ik khel , jo karta hai vo rota hai , hai yeh man ki mail"

"Surf exel haina" I typed and replied back to the sender.

It was from one of my class mate.

I opened the second message

"Hello Abhi, rem me, how r u Hun"

It was an unknown number. But I was excited. A gal or a boy came into my mind. Very patiently I typed back.

"Who's this?"

Then I opened the 3rd message

"Good night and luv u take care and don't message back"

It was a message from Priya's number. But she was not angry it seemed from her message. I didn't even try to message her back because I knew that her mobile may not beep as she had already told me several times that I should not call her or message her at night time. So I knew I have no choices except regretting and keeping patience.

Beeps

I got another message from the same unknown number.

"The gal you wanted to meet most, you forgot your angel."

I read the message and I could not control. I had to do some thing, then it came to my mind.

It was a STD number and I don't have STD facility on my number. So I didn't plan to call the sender.

So I message back:

"I know no gal and I am busy, if you are a gal please don't message me anymore now, I have turned into a **hanuman bhagat** <no to gals>"

I typed it taking a risk and keeping a stone on my heart. But I knew first impression is the last impression.

Mobile rang this time

I picked up the line.

"Hello?" I said in excitement.

'Fool fool" I hear some loud voice and laughing sounds as if I've been fooled by many people together.

"Who's this?" I ask in anger.

"It's me Rohit" from other side.

I knew I've been fooled and my message was like putting ghee in the fire.

Rohit was gonna to send my message to all and will make fun of it. Yes, Rohit my class mate, we always play pranks on each other. I really don't like this guy much.

I switched off the mobile so that I don't get fooled again now. I closed my eyes and I didn't remember when I fell asleep. And the boring day ended with a prank on me.

5
Abhi ka badla

Friends were calling me and messaging me, laughing at me, that now that I am uninterested in gals. They asked me every kind of questions like "have you started liking guys?"

"Are your hormones alright"? These things kept pissing me off. They were taking things in other way. What a bad joke it was and my life was turning hell with it. I was burning *in badle ki aag.* <Revenge>

I had to do something I had to take revenge anyhow. I call up Vicky and Ashit to have a discussion over it.

I call Ashit up "Ashit boss I really need your help please call Vicky and tell him to be at home as soon as possible"

"Okay I will be there in half an hour" replied Ashit.

I took my brunch as usual.

Bell rings.

I opened the door, no surprise Ashit and Vicky were at the door.

"What happened?" questions Vicky

"You look tense?" both ask me at once in the same tone.

"Man I need your help, Rohit played a prank on me yesterday on the phone" I told Ashit and Vicky.

"What kinda prank?" asked Ashit.

I told them the whole story and asked them if they can do anything about it. We sat on the couch planning some revenge in our mind. Everyone was silent in the room. It was not a usual sight, as we never used to be so silent, not even at examination time.

The silence broke at once. Ashit had some idea and he laughed aloud in the room like **ravana**...

Next second Ashit shouted aloud.

"Let's make a girl's account and logon to messenger"

I looked at Ashit coz I was not in a merry mood for using internet at this time.

"I have a plan" said Ashit.

I can do anything for this plan, I had it in my mind so I kept silent and watched the whole drama.

Ashit connected to the internet and in about 5 minutes after filling the messenger id form Ashit made a new profile. I kept watching him the whole time filling the form which was a girl's id.

"Julie" said Ashit.

"Julie will take your revenge" continued Ashit.

"How and who is she?" I asked Ashit

"Shut up and watch me what I am doing" said Ashit to me.

Ashit logged on the messenger and got into a chat room. Entered into a yahoo room.

"Indian room - "Delhi".

"Yes this is the destination" said Ashit again.

I could not understand anything but I kept my eyes on the computer screen to see what's happening. Ashit started typing message to boys in the room.

As we all know - Men can do anything for girls and this is a universal truth

Ashit's hand kept typing fast as if he's on border with a gun.

Bang-bang with his Ak47 speed typing.

He typed:

"Hi I am Julie"

"I am girl 32 28 32 is my size."

"Wanna be my friend"

"Call me on my personal number to be my friend"

"I'll talk to you for free."

"And much more like a bubbly gal who wana have fun with guys"

I had a smile on my face as I understood Ashit's plan now.

"Yeah it is a rocking plan" I said aloud with joy.

"Bloody fuck" came from my mouth.

And I had a big smile on my face this time, I knew it is going to work. Ashit kept trying to attract as many men as he could with this id named Julie. And typed Rohit's number repeatedly. I knew things are going to rock now with all these dirty men calling Rohit for fun and he will be pissed off with it. I start imagining that how much Rohit will be disgusted by these calls.

Guys would ask for Julie and fun, more fun…. Lol. Mission was successful and we won again. I felt satisfied now, the revenge was taken.

Hurray and it was time to celebrate. So party time.

Vicky came on computer seat now. Ashit and I were the back benchers looking at the screen. Vicky opened another escort website & started chatting. I left the room to show as if I am not interested in all this now and started watching TV for a while to my comfort.

Boys can't play with one thing for a long time I knew it; soon they will get bored and leave the house. I was still watching TV. I wanted to know about Rohit, what has happened to him and to see if my plan is successful. I could imagine his face with anger, yelling at all the wrong numbers. After an hour watching of TV, I tried Rohit's number to see what he has to say.

Did he come to know about the plot? I was wondering.

I took my mobile and looked for Rohit's number. There it was. I dialed his number.

It was switched off; I guess he might have got pissed off by the calls, that's why his number was switched off. I was laughing from inside now.

Abhi ka badla pura ho gaya tha...

The day passed like any other day now. Very next morning I woke up with my phone ringing. It was an unknown number again...

I pick it up, it was Rohit on the line, and he came to know I did this plot with him, he barked at me like a dog and said to take revenge for it. I knew him and his words but I wanted to play with him more.

A thought came to my mind.

"I have to teach you a lesson now."

He was as used words to me. I decided to do something by myself now. Rohit's friend messaged me that Rohit wanted to flash my number the very same way I did his. I have to do something quickly. I called this common friend of ours to enquire more about the situation.

He gave me Rohit's id and the take id too *"Riya"*, the boy had chosen this name to harass me. I connected to broad band and logged in to my messenger. Nothing came into my mind. I started waiting there on my chair, having my coffee. I didn't have any wish to have my brunch this time. I was on some kind of mission.

I move my eyes on screen, I saw Rohits id flashing that he is online now. I knew he was going to do something with me. An idea clicked my mind. Yeah I do have my ideas sometime it's not Ashit who is the only genius amongst us.

I registered a username like Ashit did that day, it was **"Meera"**

Meera was someone who could help me now. I typed to Rohit with this new id;

"Hi'

"Hi" replied Rohit.

He did not notice me online.

"ASL please"

I tried to be professional

"What's that" replied Rohit.

I knew Rohit does not know much about computers and I had an advantage over him.

"Means a= age, s= sex, l = location?" I type using my new id.

"Rohit, male, 21'; replies Rohit

I knew Rohit is my court now.

"Tell me yours?" asks Rohit.

Rohit knew it by name that its some girl at the other end but he was out of perception that he's been fooled again by me. I just have to make him believe and half of my work will be done.

"Am 25 f India"

"Where in India?" typed Rohit.

I knew Rohit, he could do anything to grasp a chick.

"Meera is my name" I typed.

"I can't tell you more about me coz it's dangerous for a girl to reveal her identity." I typed like a girl.

"We can be friends?" Rohit asks.

"Sure" I reply as Meera.

I typed whole stories which I have heard from girls about them and Rohit kept listening to me. I was enjoying it now. Lol it was real fun. Rohit was in my plot again now.

"I want to see u" I typed as we were friends men.

"How?" asks Rohit.

"Be on cam dumb!" I typed giving him the idea how to?

Rohit turned on his cam.

"Do u have cam?" asked Rohit

"No" I typed.

"Oh!" typed Rohit.

I knew he felt disappointed for it. I took a wild card now.

"I have a mic"; I typed.

"But I don't have mic'; typed Rohit.

Thank God Rohit was in café which don't have mic in it installed other-wise I would have been caught. In a minute or two I was able to see Rohit on cam. Bastard was smiling like he is a stud and am so much going to be impressed by him. Fellow didn't know what I was up to. I paused for a min.

"What happened?" Rohit typed.

"Nothing you're so handsome" I typed back.

"Thank you Meera" Rohit was thanked me.

Lolz.

"WC"

"??" came from other side.

"Welcome I mean" I type again being more professional.

"But there's one problem, I wanna meet you but I don't like your hair" I type.

"What is wrong with hair?" types Rohit.

"I like short hair" I reply.

Rohit had a pony tail kinda hair. He was very proud of it. I took my phone clicked a pic from the magazine and sent it to Rohit. It was a British model.

"Is this you?" typed Rohit, as if he was amazed looking at the model.

"Me? Of course" I replied.

I knew to get this dog, I had to give him a nice bone.

"Can you do something for me?" I typed.

"What?" asked Rohit.

"Wanna meet you. can't you have your hair cut before we meet? I mean it looks ugly a guy with a pony"; I typed.

"No I can't do that" typed Rohit.

It was hard for Rohit to get his hair cut, but I wanted his hair now. I wanted it desperately.

I tried to be more close to him and chat some privately till he says yes to me.

"Rohit was hard to convince about his hair cut"

I had another plan for it now. Sooner or later now, Rohit had to have a hair cut for Meera. I told him to meet me at plaza if he had a hair cut tomorrow.

I typed "bye" and tell him to be online next day.

I knew this thing would happen soon. I cut, copy paste, the whole conversation and get it printed for further use. The day passes as a beautiful day, nothing much happened that day except no calls from Priya.

She was busy with work as it was her first day at office. At late night I got a message from Priya:

"I care for u a lot, Hun, sorry could not call u and I am tired now, luv ya, good night, bye"

Ah! what ever happened today? I didn't have any time to miss Priya still I messaged back.

"Luv u and miss u a lot"

"Don't reply" I got my message back from Priya in a minute. She didn't want to have any message now. I closed my eyes and feel asleep.

Next morning I woke up and I checked my Mail and messenger. I got many messages from Rohit and, he said I wanna meet you. He had fixed time to be online.

"Come online at 11 am sharp ur Rohit"

Lol I wanted to continue, this trick with Rohit. I looked at my watch it was 10:30 am by the time. I had my brunch as fast as I could and I was ready to be online. I connected my broadband and logged on to messenger.

Messages popped into my screen.

"Hey Meera I am waitn online"

I reply back "Hi".

"Wana meet me?" A message popped in at the screen again.

"Accept the user webcam"

It was Rohit's webcam invitation. I accept it to watch the bloody bastard. To my surprise Rohit had a hair cut for me.

"Wonderful" I said to myself.

I typed "wait for me at plaza at 1:00 pm I'll b there."

I knew no one was gonna come..

I took the print out of the whole conversation we had then went to hostel with some of it's copies. I made 5 -6 copies and these were enough for me. I posted the copies to College friends too. And faxed some, mailed then and do what-ever I could do.

Friends of mine, stuck some copies to college notice board also. Rohit kept waitn at plaza but no one came. On the other side he started receiving calls again asking that where he is at the moment.

Very next day when he went to college everyone laughed at him…
I knew this thing will last for few months now.

I had my second revenge. I knew this hurt Rohit more but it was
necessary to teach him a lesson.

But every thing is fair in love and war.

It was war and I had won it. After then Rohit never called me up,
he never talked about me and never tried to be my friend again. I
kept an eye on the messenger activity from that day. Nothing
happened much from his side.

Abhi had finally won the war.

6
Lucky day

At morning following my daily routine, nothing unusual happened. I logged on to the computer connect to the internet. I check my mail and there was nothing interesting to do; I got so many mails from these porn sites which I was watching for few days. I decided to go to some escort website. To add to my difficulties my account expired and wanted more money now to have cam peck shows. I didn't care now much, nothing wonderful was happening there also.

I tried to call Priya, she didn't pick my call, as she was in office and busy with some work. Ashit and Vicky were preparing for exams, I had failed all together, and I had to wait now till bi annual to come. I was all alone again now. I kept looking at the computer screen. It was boring day.

I went to have brunch. When I come back to my room, I was

surprised to see a new friend request. It seems to be a girl's id by name.

User name was different, my hand moved towards the yes to the friend request.

Thinking this as a plot my mind was ready for the game again. I was a bit cautious. I had this feeling that Rohit might be active again for his revenge.

Something had to be done, I had to fight, and what ever is the consequence. I cannot step back to Rohit. . I took chance.

I accept the request. It was an offline request with a message. They were 3 messages in a same window.

"Hi"

"Remember me"

"See ya 7hrs later from now"

"7 from now" means I had to be online at 6 o'clock in the evening to chat with this girl.

My head started spinning, it can't be Rohit coz the body builder has to go to gym at this time and nothing in this world can stop him for it.

May be he had paid someone to do this? Some dirty thoughts kept moving in my mind. Since I had accepted the request before thinking this there was no way to repent now.

"Ok"

"Will wait' I reply.

Typing this I went offline and I switched off the computer.

I had to visit the doctor today, had an appointment.

It was a regular check up, doc wanted to have an x-ray of my foot to look for any complications.

I took a rickshaw, the clinic was near my house. Rickshaw reached the Clinic in 5 minutes or so. I waited for about half an hour, doc called me up.

We had some chit chat while he checked me up.

"Am I gonna be ok soon?" I ask doctor.

"Yes soon, plaster will be out in 3 weeks, you don't need it for long."

Just had to take care and some rest.

I was happy listening to this. As I can continue with regular activities now in 2 weeks. After the checkup and a mug of coffee I went home with my reports.

Reaching home, mom had already come back from the market. She was angry coz I had not told her and went by myself. I don't care much now. My bad times were gone now, when she had to say bad words I was in sympathy phase that now I didn't want to hear anything from anyone.

I went to my room. Lying down onto the bed, I kept thinking about this girl , who sent me friend request.

I tried remembering the user name.

"Ellenor"

I was talking to my self. I wasnt sure I had read it well. The name was looking different.

Rohit can't think of this name, looked like different one. I concluded that maybe by mistake this gal had sent me request.

Who cares, I'll not tell her and will chat with her as long as I could. Make her my friend and will continue. I'll take care of her. I can take care of every gal. Keeping it in mind I got confident now.

Priya was still busy at her office, in my heart of hearts I thought, should I share it with Priya or not.

"No" said my heart

"She'll blew upon me, may be she'll ask for my password of messenger id to check what am I doing these days."

This will mess up my fun. I decided not to tell her. Excitement was on my head.

I couldn't eat my lunch as I was badly excited. I went to my room, switched on my computer, and connected it with broadband. Put on some music and started waiting for her looking at my watch.

I was desperate to know about this girl so much that I had only half of my lunch. My eyes kept looking at screen. I was getting tired waiting for some unknown person, excitement was going down slowly.

I lay down on bed with my head towards the computer screen. I looked at my watch. It was still 5:00 o' clock. 1 hour more, came to my mind.

At this time I didn't want Ashit or Vicky to call me or disturb me. Neither did I want Priya to interfere nor my dad to call me up for a talk or so. I closed my door. Bolt it well for privacy.

Beep

I looked at the screen. There was one message on the screen. I prayed to God that it should not be Priya's message and no message which can give me tension at this moment.

Priya seemed to be less important to me. To braced myself, I stopped thinking about her and continued to work.

I opened the message:

"State result is out, give Ur roll no and send to 6670 to get Ur result'

This message was of no use to me, I deleted it and for the first time I was so happy with such kind of advertisement message.

I switched off the mobile so that no one disturbs me. Slowly the time came, it was 6 o'clock now. I had this girl in my mind. Sooner or later she will be chatting with me and I was happy with this thought.

Time has finally come to chat with the girl and I started thinking about her, I talked to myself:

saala bolunga kya <What to talk>

While thinking about the punch line and in a thought of impressing the girl I forgot to look at computers screen. To my surprise there were 3 messages on the screen repeatedly hitting "buzz" to get my attention.

"Oh" I cried my self blaming for not looking at the screen.

"Hi" I typed in a second.

"What Ur doing?" message came from other side.

"Nothing was just waiting for some mail" I typed.

Just to make her sure I was not waiting for her and this might ruin my first impression.

"Oh ok" came the message with reply.

"Must be busy then I'll catch u later" second message beeped with the first one.

May be net was slow that's why message came together. One thing was sure that this was not Rohit, other wise he won't show me such a cold shoulder.

It was some one different with some different attitude. And I was enjoying this mysterious girl. To continue the chat I asked her about what she did for the whole day. Very casually she answers me the same routine which we all follow.

I still did not know about this girl and how she has this id of mine. She kept chatting with me with a new guy. If it was someone known she might have asked old things. But she was enquiring about me. So I was sure this girl was new to me and she didn't even know me much.

To confirm this now I asked her for her introduction.

70

"Don't you remember?"

"To how many girls have you passed your id"

"It hit me like an arrow"

She type and I didn't expect such reaction at the moment from her.

"No really I don't remember anyone and I usually don't talk much on internet and I am surprised to see your friend request" I typed back to sort out things.

"Guess who?" the girl went cheesy this time.

"Whom did u last time gave your id?" she asked me.

I could not remember anything. I was confused with this question.

"No one" I said.

"Ok let's end it then"

"I expected a lot from u" said the girl from other side.

"U gave me your id to the website I had been working, U talked to me nicely that's y I ask u on my yahoo account otherwise I usually don't talk much to guys" she introduced herself in a pissed off way.

"To the website working for, Oh my God"

This was the girl from the escort's website

Oh man!

Was I with that charming gal chatting on messenger I could hardly believe myself and my luck.

"Sorry I am really busy these days that's why I didn't remember you" I typed to make her understand.

"You know I don't visit your website too." I continued.

"Yes that's why I came here. How are you?" she replied back.

"How's life going?' she continued again.

"Good"

"Nothing much to do" I replied.

"I have a foot fracture and I am going through tough time recovering." I typed it in such a manner to gain some sympathy because this was needed at this moment to gain her attention.

"Ok well are you ok now?" she enquired.

"Then it must be bad?." she starts showing me some care which I was planning to get.

"No it is not, till you are there for me to chat." I replied in a bit flirty way.

"So can I ask you your A.S.L AGAIN? " I change the topic.

"But this time in a serious mood, not like the website. Gimme your info but it must be real." I ask her like a gentleman.

"Ok."

"My name is Ellenor"

"I am from U.S"

"I am Arts student and I work for the website for part time for my pocket money."

All these messages came with her introduction. She was trying to clear herself

"Are you an art student?" I asked in a surprise.

My eyebrow was raised. I could not expect it coz I thought she's a professional call girl working for a website. I was still not sure whatever she had said might be true or not. Who cares, I was talking to a girl and it was enough for me.

So tell me more about you and your family.

I show some concern. I live with my mother and she's divorced. That was something usual as we know Americans don't believe in relations much.

"Ok sorry I didn't know that" I replied being more of a gentle man. I was trying to impress this girl

"Ok it's ok" she reply back in a casual way.

"Tell me about the weather there, It's hot here" I change the topic to lighten the mood.

"It's hot here" said the girl.

"Same here" I replied.

Then we went on about some global warming and all those intellectual issues. I was a medical student but this time I was enjoying the science of arts.

She was really a good student coz she was typing at good speed with good knowledge

I had opened wikipedia for it so that I could impress her more and talk with her more. I knew I had made a good impression on her. All I have to do is to maintain it more. I talked to her nicely and sincerely.

Time passed so quickly with her. Then suddenly she said she had to go. It was a heart breaking moment but the chat had to end anyhow.

"When to meet u next" I questioned.

"Same time tomorrow" reply came from other side.

I came to knew that the girl was interested to talk more.

"Ok" I said in a manner as if I'm not so keen, hiding my emotions.

We men know it how to play with a gal.

(bhav do par itna na do ki vo khud ko hurpari samjhne lagge)

It was 9 o'clock now.

We exchanged good night with each other.

I was tired also. It was dinner time too. I switched on my mobile.

2 Messages came onto the screen

It was Priya's message

I opened first message

"Hi dude lot of work at office so that I could not message u"

Don't mind, me too busy I myself thought.

Then I opened second message

"No message from your side either even no miss call"

So Priya hadn't check my phone status whether I was switched off or not

I typed message "went to the doctor dear that's y I was bit busy whole day came home late" sent it to her

Mom called me up for dinner. I went out leaving the phone there.

Having my dinner I didn't even remember the phone was on silent so Priya called me up 3-4 times after my message to ask me how was meeting with doc.

I was a bit careless but Priya will not say anything if I'll call her up now. It was just 20 min after she called.

I called her up but she didn't pick up phone. Might be sleeping I lied down onto the bed and when did my eyes closed, I didn't really remember.

7

When trouble starts

Everything was fine from my side.

Finally the date sheet came. I had to appear for my supplementary examination.

It was now two weeks that I and Ellenor were chatting on internet.

Friends seemed to be unimportant now.

I started visiting central library for 8 hours from morning till evening so that I can have time to chat with Ellenor. She seemed to be pretty interesting more than Priya back den. Priya and I often than usual to talk less. May be her job was getting hectic or I was ignoring her but the thing was that I was enjoying my life. Priya used to call me but I had silly reasons to ignore her thing that I have an examination to appear for, so she has to give me some time to study, for me it was time to spend with Ellenor.

Ellen and I, yes I call her Ellen now, she and I were good friends now. We had started a new relationship where we talked to each other everyday discussing our routine activities and all.

8th august 7:30 pm

Usual timing, I and Ellen were chatting.

"Hi" typed Ellen.

"Hello babes" to be frank with her, yes I had become very frank with this American girl. We could talk everything including sex now. These things were so casual for her and me.

"Guess what?" typed Ellen.

"What" I typd replying her.

My inner instincts were telling me that something bad was going to happen to me one day. The thing was I was ignoring Priya a lot.

I thought she did know about Priya. Then I thought at once how she can know about her. I had never talked about Priya with her. Now she was my G.F. on the net.

"I got certificate on tattoo making" typed Ellen.

"Congrats" I type.

So this was I who was creating imaginary trouble, Ellen was like every dumb gal who used to share every single bit of their life. May be girls get happiness by this but boys used to remain silent for all these stuff.

To add more to her happiness, I added "When am I going to get your name tattood on my body Hun" I was expecting some lame excuse from her. But things were different this time. The bad storm was chasing me right away.

"Soon when I'll travel to India"

I asked to myself. "Is she going to come?"

Then in my heart's heart I thought this is good enough to enjoy, if she's going to visit India then we'll party all together and have fun. But then I looked at my pocket it was saying don't call her up man I can't put up with all these expenses.

Then to inquire more I asked her.

"When and how you're coming here?" I typed back to Ellen.

"Hun I told you that I was doing art course from my university"

"They want me to study culture, so I decided to study Indian culture and this is how I can visit and meet you also." Answer came from the other end.

"This would be nice and you'll take care of me too." I typed got worried this time.

Great!!

I said to myself, well never mind if I need this American gal with me, I have to do something for it also.

"You know what I would be getting scholarship for it?" typed Ellen.

"Sure I'll wait for you" I typed.

"I'll be visiting India in Jan" replied Ellen, and her answer was full of excitement.

"Ok, I'll arrange everything for you till then" I typed back ending the conversation.

It was a good plan on my part as my exams would be finishing till then. I'll have hell lot of time to spend with her.

Priya was busy with work, never mind and who is going to tell her about what I am up to. Whereas things will be fine, this American girl would be back to her place leaving sweet memories and some good experience too. Thinking this made me very comfortable and my inner conscious also allowed me to go ahead and meet her.

Beep

It was message from Priya: "I'll be going to Delhi".

Nothing else was written there so to enquire more I called her up.

Ringing

Every ring was making me nervous.

After two calls, Priya picked up my call.

"Hey Priya what's this, why your going to Delhi?" I said in a single breath about enquiringwhat she said.

I was not liking it that Priya was going away from me. This was a hard moment for me.

"This is for my industrial classes" replied Priya and her voice sounded as if she was excited.

I wanted to be with Priya but she was going.

"Is it necessary Priya? I wanted to be with you?" I replied back in a kid dish way as I knew it well that this was important to impress her.

Priya could easily find me in tears and she could find it in my voice that how much I was going to miss her. But it was also necessary to tell her that I want her to be with me.

"Will you be in contact with me?" I asked in a worrying way.

"Of course, why you are saying like this?" she replied back.

"Distances can make relations apart" I said with a sad voice.

"Its not the distances from the miles, its distances from the heart which makes people away." Priya said it to me to make me feel comfortable as my words were making it clear that I was bit unhappy about her going away.

It was the first time in my relation Priya had supported and talked like a brave girl.

I was happy about it but was sad too. Priya knew I have exams on the way and she would be leaving me, this will also affect my exams. Moreover I am going to miss her more and I'll be in pain. That was going to hamper my studies too.

"Don't worry I'll call you every day but you study for your exams" said Priya bravely.

But no words from Priya could stop me from being insecure.

Yes I was insecure about Priya coz I had heard often that people forget their loved ones while they are away.

"I'll be moving in a week" said Priya, breaking the silence.

"Ok" I replied back to hide my true feelings and to show myself to be secured and brave.

"I'll give my exam and will visit you" I said.

"Ok but first concentrate on your studies" Priya tried to change the topic and the tension which had been created.

But I wanted to discuss it more, so didn't to change the topic continued "We'll spend some good time together before you leave. So that you can take along some sweet memories."

But this time Priya was also not in a good mood and she said "We'll think over it".

Her uninterested answer made me furous and what I wanted at that moment she couldn't understand! I really wanted to fight with my girl for no good reason. She was going and I didn't like it, so I wanted to talked arrogantly.

Sometimes we talk nicely but sometimes it is necessary to fight to make the other person miss you a lot.

"You may leave tomarrow?" I said, to add on to the fight and my anger.

Priya did not like my question so she hung up the phone and only what I could hear was buzzing sound in my ear.

This made me even more furious and to add more to the heat I messaged her.

"I know this is what's going to happen, when you will be gone, you will not call me, no more you will ignore me".

No response came from her side.

I watched the screen of my mobile for next 2 days and I knew my message did hurt Priya a lot, but this time I didn't care for her feelings I only cared for mine.

Finally the time came for Priya to leave for Delhi and we still didn't had any contact. That was the final moment, the fight had to end and finally one of us had to reconcile the matter. But this is time it was gonna be not I was strident me. I had decided it, the earlier that day of the fight so I kept silent.

Beep

It was Priya's message on my mobile. I opened it

"Abhi I am going, please I want to see you before I go."

I could easily find the agony in the message. My heart also felt the same, the way Priya would have felt at the time when she had typed the message.

Finally I decided to end the fight, so I typed the message.

"Sorry for the fight, Priya let's meet then"

Reply came in a moment.

"I can't meet honey I am packing my stuff but I can come to my balcony you just come and let me see you before I go."

It was short but sweet message but packing and for this reason she wasn't gonna meet me disappointed.

I would be going but I wound up mess something decided.

I typed the message, "Okay I'll give you buzz when I'll come then you can to the balcony."

While typing it had decided to make something happens, so that I could see her but she wouldn't able to see and miss the change and this will make her feel hurt for not having the chance.

I kicked my scooter and reached on the road below her balcony I knew she would be waiting for my call, so I went into a nearby shop and stood there and gave her buzz.

Priya came from the room and stood in the balcony I could easily see my girl and I could easily make out her eyes searching for me. I kept looking at her, standing for a while she took her mobile from the pocket and dialled my number. This was something I wanted.

I didn't pick call. She kept standing there for a while and I just gazed her from the shop only, with out any reply. Then after some time Priya went back in.

I knew she was felt disgraced but I don't know why I wanted it happen. I wanted her to be despised.

I went back home and called up. Priya picked the call and in a low voice uttered "Where were you? I was there at balcony for so long!"

Priya was still expecting to see me, but I was uninterested and was happy to win over the fight.

"I came and looked at balcony could find no one here so I guessed there must be some my judgement, better luck next time" I said.

Priya did get hurt, but she said nothing to me. I even kept silent.

"I am going, and I don't know why you are doing this to me at this very moment?" asked Priya.

"Take care of your self." I replied.

I knew Priya was in train and she kept calling me to talk but I still didn't pick her calls. I knew I was doing wrong but I don't know why I was doing all this.

The days passed by and from the very next morning I started preparing for my examination.

8
Why we always fight

After days of hard work, it was now time for me to give my exams.

Finally I was all prepared like a soldier to be in examination hall.

I tried Ellen's number so that I could get her wishes.

I couldn't make a call, as I was short of balance.

It was sad; I wanted Ellen to wish me.

I had chatted with her last evening but was missing her like hell.

Sliding cell phone into my pocket, I started moving towards the examination hall.

There was still 15 minutes to go.

Ellen might called; she knew that I had an exam.

Beep

Phone vibrated in my pocket.

"Best of luck for the exam cutie pie, do well follow instructions carefully"

It was Priya I could easily recognize her, giving me instructions like my mom.

Why does she thinks I am a kid?

I got a bit irritated by this message.

I knew I was wrong but I needed space, I didn't want her to keeping tell me everything always and every time. I am not a kid, infuriated I typed back "I know everything" and sent her the message.

Message shook me up again in a minute

I was still expecting Ellen to contact me.

"Why do we always fight?"

This message from Priya, made me think of her.

What I am doing to her? and how much does she care for me?

It skanced & kind demused that why I did wait for someone who is not in my life? and virtually ignoring the person I had in my life for real?

Oh God!!

I was in tears right there.

I felt deeply care and love for Priya that I could not express it.

I texted her again.

"My lucky charm, we fight coz we love each other"

I knew this was enough to express.

I switched off the mobile and went into the examination hall.

That time my feelings were pure and were for Priya. I thought of forgetting everything for Ellen. I knew she was fake and I was fake for her either.

"The thing was my love was never fake."

But in Ellen's case it was love? Love is something which can turn your world upside down... Something which gives you relief when you are in pain… something in explicable... Something like a treasure in the world of hypocrites... Love was something I had for Priya.

After spending two hours in examination hall, and writing some good answers on my answer sheets it was time for me to enjoy.

Varun and Manav were there waiting for me outside the examination hall onto his bike. Yes they were there, for me, coz now it was time to party. We had to drink, we had to puff.

This is life. I was back on the track.

I went with them the very moment into the nearest bar to have a mug of beer to chill. There we talked a lot, about us and our life. They were busy with their internship.

So I was left alone.

Manav while taking last sip of the beer announced "I am moving out."

"Am going to U.S."

"Why the hell are u leaving us, aren't u happy here?" said Varun.

"Yes" I too agreed with him.

"My father wants me to go, that's why" replied Varun.

"Take care of my things Abhi" said Manav in a sad tone.

I knew what he was talking about. He was talking about his G.F. Through an eye contact he could tell me to take care of her. I knew what he meant so I nodded gently. The discussion ended with Varun keeping against the chair while he was trying to ask for the payment slip. And we all had a heartly caugh we forgot the seriousness of the situation.

As Manav was moving abroad, he had planned to do things on his own way. Few friends were left back. I kept thinking all the way, what life is, why did he meet us and shared moments with us, if we had to part. Thinks about it all made me numb. Reaching home, I just remembered to switch on my phone, I immediately switched on my mobile, it was time that I thought about Ellen.

She might have tried my number.

This Ellen thing was getting me into it more and more and I had just started thinking of her very much, may be I was addicted to her. Nothing from her side, Ellen didn't even message me.

I lay even on the bed and I fell asleep so deeply that I didn't remember to close the door. And when I opened my eyes, mother was back at home and was yelling at me about my attitude towards life. How irresponsible I am towards things and how careless I am. Nothing seem important at that moment.

I looked at the mobile. There was still some time.

Yes, still time I could manage to catch up with Ellen.

It was 7:30pm she might be online. I got online within a second. Yes she was there on messenger.

"Hi" I typed.

"Fine" Ellen replied.

"So what's new in life?" typed Ellen again.

"Nothing much" I typed casually.

"You know what I passed my assignment to work on culture of India" typed Ellen with delighted.

I could understand that she was happy and obliged at the moment coz it was a big thing for her but what about me? I had my exam and she didn't even bother to say good luck.

"I had my exam today" I typed.

"Oh I am sorry I totally forgot, but I know u will get better marks than anyone" typed Ellen.

Better than anyone? she didn't even knew that I had a supplementary. But I kept my anger to myself. Ellen was special to me and I didn't want to hurt her as I had already made a lot of plans as she was moving to India.

So I wanted to spend time with her, and it was not the right time to make her feel bad about anything.

I needed her here. So I said nothing to her at the moment.

"When are you coming?" I coming exact to the point. I asked.

"January" she replied elated.

She didn't knew what I had been going through. How I felt?

"Ok" I typed.

To end the conversation I started typing slowly so that she might get mad off at me. I didn't want to talk to her, at least not today. Yes I was happy that she was coming but I was upset coz she didn't wish me.

Beep

Mobile vibrated on the bed.

I looked at it, it was Priya.

"Hey *jaan* today is 2ⁿᵈ" don't you remember it dear, the special day"

The message was sweet but it was taunting me. I switched off the computer after typing the last bye that net was slow, so couldn't talk and would had disconnect any time.

"I do remember it Hun, was waiting for the time, I was bit tired you know it **Na**:" I messaged her back.

After it Priya didn't say anything, I knew I had to call her up, have a good talk with her. She was my girl, the girl of who ruled my dreams.

I picked up my phone called her up but got no reply. Priya was disappointed by my same ignoring attitude. She knew I will never feel the same way she feels. May be I was wrong in my dealings but I am a guy and guy's are always the same you never changing.

They don't talk much but they feel the same way girls do.

More over guys don't cry they only cry when they are stridently hurt.

I was sad too for the thing only that all I could do is to say sorry to my girl to get things right.

I called Priya again but still got no reply. I wanted to talk to her badly now.

"Please pick up my call, it's urgent" I typed the message to Priya so that she might get panicked but at least she will pick my call.

To my surprise this thing really worked. This time in a single ring Priya took my call.

"Hello" said Priya from the other side.

Her voice was numb but she took my call coz she was worried about what was worrying me?

She cared for me a lot? I knew it.

"Hi" I replied back

"What happened?" asked Priya in a worried.

"Nothing" I said.

I was laughing and Priya was furious this time.

"Abhi I don't like this kind of jokes, these could take my breath out of me" said Priya.

"Sorry jaan" I just wanted to wish you and you were not picking up my call" I said.

"Time is running out wish me, jaldi se, else 3rd ho jayegi, wish me up" says Priya in a jolly way so to change the topic so that we don't fight.

"Happy 2nd" I said.

"And keep loving me and reminding me every 2nd of my life" continued I.

"One day when I would leave then you would cry for this 2nd and would want to wish me" replied Priya, in a serious way.

"You won't not do anything like this" I said confidently.

"One day I would" said Priya again.

But who cared, for time being, everything was fine and things were going well.

"Shut up feel the silence" said I and the topic got changed from a tense to a romantic one.

The line was silent and we both could hear each other breaths and by time they got heavier and heavier and we could hardly remember when line the line cut and we fell asleep.

In the morning when I woke up I typed message to Priya

"I promise to visit you there in a week or two"

This is how life got settled and another fine 2nd passed by.

9
Sharing love

Life got settled a bit coz after the last message typed to Ellen was really a last message, I don't know she got annoyed by me, but the thing was she was offline and said that she would be busy with the report, for the whole month I planned to spend some time with Priya.

Yes, I was going to Delhi for 5 days and these 5 days I was going to spend each and every moment with Priya.

This was special and I started packing.

Train tickets were booked on time.

Priya and me we didn't had a talk since past one week.

So to a surprise her, I called up.

Rings

No one answered.

I knew she might be busy with work but I had a good news to give so I was little excited for it too.

I tried her number again and again but no reply from other side.

So the plans changed a little. Now it was going to be a surprise visit.

Everything was going fine now.

It was time to cherry love and it was time to merry my relation.

I had to do shopping for Priya.

I wanted to have some flowers for her, may be a bunch of 21 Red Roses might be good enough to make her feel special, I thought in my mind.

Something more other than flowers, more romantic, I decided at that moment.

It was bit confusing but I wanted it to be very romantic when I'd meet her.

So time had come, I was going after 2 days.

I searched net for something crazy, I could do for my G.F. Nothing really special striked my mind till I had this idea of anklets.

Anklets, it was something I was really searching for.

Days were long and nights were longer to spend without calling her.

I tried her number every day but no response came.

Finally I reached Delhi, still trying her number with no response from other side.

This time I knew Priya would be mad at me.

I type message to her

"This is important"

Reply came from other side within a second

"Am busy message me what is important"

"I am in Delhi want to meet"

"Not now go somewhere else I'll call u up when free"

This was something I was expecting, finally I was meeting her.

I went to my friends place…

Days passed but no reply, finally at 7:00 pm evening, mobile beeps.

I jumped out of my bed; I knew it was Priya's message

There was a message from Priya.

"Come to PVR Priya's market will wait for you there at 7:30.

"Where is Priya Market" I asked my friend.

"It a bit far away from here you will get bus for it and if u want to reach there soon go by some private means."

I have to reach soon so everything got decided in my mind in a single second.

I got ready packed and went downstairs to get convenience.

My friend followed me to say bye but I was in a bit hurry.

"Your stuff Abhi" reminded my friend.

"Oh! Anklets" said I, the thing totally gone out of my mind in excitement.

"Thanks" I replied putting the anklets in my pocket.

I needed flowers so I had to be in a hurry.

It was my every day problem that I don't keep my things simple and easy and in the end I always have to run.

Getting into Auto-rickshaw "take me to PVR Priya Market"

In a moment we were heading towards to the destination.

I kept looking outside for a flower shop.

"I have to had some flowers too" I said to driver.

"Ok Babuji" said the driver.

On a red light crossing we got these flowers too, but the thing was Delhi is so packed with cars what ever you do you will definitely land up into a traffic jam.

So finally I was wasting time in traffic.

I got hyper now, but nothing could be done.

I called priya.

"Hey I am in traffic I think I'll not reach at time, will you wait for me?"

"Ya sure never mind, but do try to come soon am alone here waiting"

This made me more tensed, my girl was waiting for me alone in a new place and I was here sitting.

Finally I reached at Priya market after some time may be 15 minutes late or so.

Priya's face was cherry red and she was bit upset.

I jumped out of the Rickshaw with a big smile on my face and flowers in my hand so that she won't have any words to say.

Looking at flowers the redness of her face just faded in a second. Priya really loved flowers, I knew it.

All her anger vanished and we started to walk while I looked in to her eyes.

She was so happy to see me.

"You rascal, why didn't you tell me that you are coming?" said Priya.

"Hey I tried to call you number of time" I answered in a witty manner.

"You would blame me that I don't pick calls and then you will say look I came from so far for you and you didn't meet me" said Priya in a loving way.

"I don't need excuses ok lets move from here and go to some place, where we are alone" I said.

"No let's have coffee" said Priya.

"Ok" I replied.

Then we started moving towards the coffee shop.

While we were moving our hands were touching each other's hand.

It was a soothing feeling, in a second touch or two, I put my little finger into her little finger and the bond of love got shared.

I held her hand it was a magical moment... I got same response from Priya's side too, she also held my hands at the same time and we went in to the coffee shop holding each others hand.

Entering the coffee shop was so romantic.

Lights were bit dim with sweet music, just the way I wanted at this moment.

We went upstairs so that we could talk alone.

As we reached the first floor it was full with love birds. As Delhi is **dillwalo ki**.

While sitting I was still in a confused state when and how to make the move.

I had those anklets in my hands now all I had to do was to give her but crazy thoughts kept buzzing in my mind.

Now it was decided by me that I'll not give anklets to her but rather I'll bend down and tie them myself.

I bent down but thinking for everyone watching me I sat up again.

Priya kept watching me and found that something was there that I was hiding and she could feel my discomfort.

"What are you hiding" Priya asked me with a smile on her face, as if she knew I have something for her.

"Nothing" I replied.

"Don't hide" asked Priya.

"Well there's something Priya but this isn't the right place" said I.

"If the thing is special then the place is right too and if you want me to see it, then I want to see it now." ordered commanded.

"Okay" I said while bending down but I could not reach.

"You can sit with me", said Priya.

I went to the other side of the table and beside her.

It was easy now but I didn't want to bend now, coz I had done it thrice without suceeding.

"Can you sit with your leg crossed or over leg?" I asked.

"Ok" said Priya while sitting the way I asked her to.

The very moment she did this, I tied the anklet on her ankle with a smile on my face.

"That's for you honey" said I.

"Now how about the second one?" asked I.

Priya could not say anything, the scene was so emotional that she kept staring at me and I could find the aura feeling for me.

That was awesome the way I wanted to be. All I wanted from her was hear love you. I kept watching her lips if they move a bit for uttering the golden words.

I could read her lips saying Love you.

I said "Keep repeating"

This continued till the coffee came and the eye contact broke.

Priya was feeling so shy she could hardly look at me while she was busy stirring her coffee.

An hour passed and we couldn't about talk anything...

Then it was time to depart, I felt heart broken and didn't want to leave, but it was the thing I had to do.

After payment of me the bill and we moved out was different, I was moved ahead and Priya followed.

We both were shy.

While moving out of market, finally it was time to depart and I had to take an auto rickshaw.

"Wait a minute" voice finally came from Priya's mouth.

She wanted to say something.

I was expecting something like- don't go or love you.

"Where is the other anklet?" enquired Priya.

It was still with me right there in my pocket.

"Abhi other anklet?" said Priya.

"You lost it some where" I said.

"This is not done, you don't care for my things!" I exclaimed.

"No really Abhi" Priya was in tears then, she didn't want to loose it at any cost.

"Let's see there at other places together" I said.

I knew the anklet was there in my pocket.

The continue the mischief I went inside again to the coffee shop with Priya.

"So where did u lose it?" I asked.

"I don't remember Abhi" said Priya with a soft voice in a guilty manner.

Moving to the other side of the market, it was a pretty lonely place and there was a fountain.

"Sit here and let me check where it is" I said in bossy way.

Priya sat on the bench saying nothing.

I bent down taking anklet from my pocket and tied it on her ankle.

Priya still unaware of the thing I was up to.

"Abhi what are you doing?" Priya asked in a tense way.

"So here is your anklet darling"; I said.

Priya with a big smile looked at me as if she found some treasure.

I laughed at her while Priya was in tears.

"You cheated me and now you are laughing" Priya shouted at me.

"This is not done Abhi!" bursted Priya.

"This is too much!" she continued.

And when I stood up I could not guess when I went into Priya's arm and we hugged each other tightly.

Finally the lovable date ended with a lovely hug.

As the days went by we had great talks on the phone as she could not meet me coz of her office work.

Finally the day came when I had to move back and I went home leaving Priya.

10
Chasing a Storm

It was January, climate was cold and so was my mind these days.

Going out with Priya had changed my mind and had diverted my mind towards her again. And it was absently as an ectasy.

I began thinking that I had fallen in love with Priya again.

Nothing in this world could ever make me happy the way I could be while I'm with my G.F.

Yes it was true, coz she cares for me a lot.

And who doesn't want to cared for his life, every one want it a little or a lot.

Everything was going fine; Ellen was now out of my mind until this

Phone rang...

It was an unknown number with id masking as if it was an I.S.D number, calling from some computer internet call... Skype or something.

I was driving and on my way home from my friend's b'day party.

I picked up the call while driving.

"Hello" I said while picking up the call.

"Hi it's me Ellenor" the voice was somehow not familiar but the accent was something I could guess it was not an Indian who ever was calling.

"Yes who's this?" I enquired, I still could not recognize the name and the person coz I was still busy driving.

"Guess then you should know me better!" reply came from other side.

I was sure now who ever was calling knew me well.

"Ok lemma take some time as I am driving too so please call me after 20 minutes I'll be at home and will talk to you then." I said all these in a single breath and banged down the mobile and concentrated on driving.

The mobile kept beeping while I was driving back home.

I looked at the screen there were around 10-15 calls I dint pick up.

I opened the miss call list.

I was expecting Priya to give me missed call because after I always used to call her for hours so we can have some lovely talks.

But to my surprise no calls came from Priya, it was all from that unknown number.

I went to bathroom to fresh myself up and put the phone onto the computer table.

While washing my face, I felt the phone vibrating on the table.

I went out to see who is calling.

It was again the same number.

"Ya tell me who is this? else I'll not talk' I said.

"It's me Ellen from America" the voice was bit sad this time.

The charm in the voice before at the first call was gone.

"I called you up to give you a surprise that I am coming to India but I think you have forgotten me, your chat friend" she said all this so that I could remember something about her.

I was not expecting her at all.

I was into good relation with Priya and I didn't want her to be with me now. The entire craze for her was gone.

It was merely an infatuation I had for her, but the person I loved was Priya and I could not think of anyone else at all these days.

"Ok hi Ellen, I thought you are gone and" I said.

"How could I forget you Hun bunny?" "Ellen interrupted me in a passionate way.

Hunny-bunny, Ellen used to call me such names when ever she's in a mood to flirt. But I was not in a mood today.

I wanted Priya to call me.

"So what's up I am coming to India, I'll make a tattoo for you?" said Ellen

"Onto your chest, onto your heart be prepared for it" continued Ellen.

Tattoo was not the problem; it was Ellen who was the problem.

"When are you coming?" I enquired.

"This week only or may be a bit later but I would message you and I would be there just for you" replied Ellen.

"Where you going to stay?" I enquired again.

"Delhi is my destination!" replied Ellen.

Delhi fuck man! Priya is also there I can't meet her like this in open, she might see me.

I don't want to take any risk.

While I was thinking all this, Priya's call was beeping on the call waiting.

I wanted this talk to end here but couldn't do, Ellen was calling from America and I can't say her to drop the line like this. I have to speak to her until she drops the line herself.

Priya might get angry if it happened over and over, I said to myself.

Nothing could be done now. Ellen was coming to India for me and on my faith.

I will have to help her in any case.

"I'll manage everything, it's from my university only" said Ellen.

"All you have to do is to meet me and rest I'll take care of you" she continued.

This thing gave me a shiver and in a moment I agreed to meet her, the old feelings took over me again. The devil in me had risen again.

Let me check what she meant by take care of you...

It was mischievous and I liked mischiefs.

Priya will not know I thought.

All I have to do is make up some good excuse to tell my mom and dad so that they can send me to Delhi for the trip again as I had one last month.

And I knew dad was not going to send me there again at any cost.

So what ever was to be told, should had been bold enough so that they can't say no to me.

"Ok Hun, I have to leave now for the ticket counter, will message you regarding it" Ellen dropped the line while saying this.

I could not say proper bye to her.

I looked at the screen; Priya had called me several times.

She wanted to talk.

I was excited about Ellen, so I called Priya up to cheer her, but not in a same mood I had before to talk.

I just wanted to say hi and end the call soon.

"Hello" said my angel.

"Hi Priya sorry for not picking your call it was my senior calling me, as you know I have to start internship that's why" I said covering my self

"No worries actually I was busy too, so I can't talk much now, tell me how was your day" says Priya.

This was what I wanted, a short talk and the cute one.

"Days are long and empty without you" I tried to **lagaao makkhan** this time.

"Ok don't worry I am there for you" replied Priya.

"Are you wearing the anklets I gave you" I said.

"Ya I am, they remind me of you, just can't wear them at office but rest of the day I wear them," Priya said in a romantic way.

"Ok" I had no other thing to talk now.

I was thinking of something else, Ellen.

I was thinking about Ellen.

How to meet her?

How to impress her and all?

The line was silent for few minutes.

Priya was busy with her work, but she wanted me to say something to her...

"Ok I'll have to put down the phone now, will talk to you later" said Priya.

"Ok Hun never mind" I said.

What had happened to me? I didn't even know myself.

Why I was so happy and so excited, I did not even know whether a storm was chasing me or it was me who was chasing a storm.

Line went off but the phone was still held in a listening position.

Now it was confirmed that Ellen is visiting India and I am going to meet her.

16 January.

At morning, phone vibrated, early in the morning.

"Hello" sounds familiar from other side.

"Hello! Who is this?" I replied.

"Good morning, Wake up "someone said from other side.

Before I could say anything the voice sounded like an American accent.

"Who is it you? Ellen?" I said.

"Ya Hunny bunny it's me" replied Ellen from other side.

"Yeah! How come you called me up so early in the morning?' I asked Ellen taking a yawn.

I was expecting Ellen to call me up.

"Be ready to meet me dear I am coming on 20th this month." said Ellen.

"Meet me at Delhi I would not be able to call you for some days" continued Ellen as if she was my G.F.

I didn't like this attitude of her. She was thinking that Delhi is in my neighborhood. All I have to do is put my shoes on and walk a mile and be there.

I was bit irritated by this nature of her's but as I had promised her to meet, so I decided to make a plan to meet Ellen.

The thing now was, I had to go.

I had to make a plan out so.

I called Manav to rescue me.

Rings

"Hi! Manav. This is me Abhi" I said at once when Manav picked up the call.

"Oh hi, Abhi how come you remembered me today so early in the morning?" replied Manav.

I need some help buddy.

I told Manav the whole story, how I got Ellen on net and then about her visit to India and her plan to meet me. Manav kept listening; maybe he was shocked about what I had beendoing in my life. It was like slipping into fire, but being a good friend Manav asked me "What do you want meet do".

"Need a plan to go to Delhi for a week or so" I said.

"Let me think I'll call you after an hour" Manav replied.

I got up from my bed and went to the bathroom to freshen up and started thinking for myself if I could have an idea other than Manav.

Finally Manav called me up.

"So Abhi, I think if I asked convinience you wanted go for internship from there and you have to go to Delhi at some big institute for being recommended for it, might help you out for it" Manav said.

His idea was good, I gave a thought. This might help me and if Manav would help me out in it and will talk to Mom and Dad for it, it would be better.

"So give a call and talk to Mom and Dad for it" I said.

This was something I knew will be tough to convince Manav to talk to Mom and Dad and lie in front of them as expected Manav denied to do so.

Finally I needed someone to help me out. I called Varun up for this.

"Help me, if you are a true friend" I said to Varun, it was something like black mailing him for the friendship and I knew this will work.

"Ok I can try but I can't assure you that it would work" replied Varun.

I knew if Varun would convince, things will work.

Finally at noon Varun talked to Mom and Dad and convinced them.

So I was ready and all packed up to board to Delhi.

There were days for me to got Delhi and I concentrated on Manav's trip to U.S.

It was a sad departure. Finally Manav was gone, I remained sad for few days till my time came to go to Delhi. By the time I received calls from Priya but I ignored her telling I have to give time to Manav as he was going out and will catch her sometime after Manav will board.

Priya did understand I needed to spend some time with Manav so she remained silent.

Finally time came, I was going to Delhi again, without telling Priya.

There was risk on my side so I told Varun not to tell Priya about anything.

Varun promised me not to tell anything to Priya and the Delhi trip started.

Varun asked me again if I was doing the right thing but nothing could stop me that moment. No matter were the consequences.

11
Ship wrecked

—20 January 9 a.m.—

Finally, the day came to meet Ellen. I was in Delhi at my friend's place. I had already lied to him telling him that I was going to meet some of my relative and would be sharing his room for the day.

At morning my Friend was out for work and I was all alone in the room.

Phone rings

It was some local number and was unexpected. I had totally forgotten that Ellenberg in India had a local number.

"Hi" it was Ellen's call.

"Hi" I replied.

By the time I had recognized Ellen's voice.

"I am here at Delhi" I continued.

I was all prepared to meet Ellen.

"So where are we going to meet?" asked Ellen.

I knew nothing about Delhi so I had to consult some one for it.

"Where are you now and where do you want to meet me?" I asked Ellen.

"I am at my hotel" Ellen replied.

"Ok lets meet at your hotel then we'll go somewhere for the dinner" I suggested making a good plan from my side.

"Ok with me" said Ellen as she was eager to meet me.

We both knew what was going to happen in the room and still we were pretending that we are innocent enough hiding our sexual feelings. I was bit uncomfortable about the thought.

—@—

—Reaching at hotel—

I enter the hotel. My hands were cold now. It was something I had never done before.

I had cold shiver thinking about what could happen between Ellen and me. My stomach was aching about the experience I am going through. As I reach the enquiry desk my heart sank and I had cold sweat. I knew this is the destination I had been searching for.

Priya's thought was out of the mind. All I was thinking about was Ellen. I knew I had been doing was wrong on my part but sometimes these things seemed to be fair enough.

"Good after noon sir what can I do for you?" said the girl on the desk.

Her sweet voice broke my silence. I came into my senses. I have to ask for the Ellen's room, came into my mind.

"Ya hi "I reply in a confusing manner.

I took my mobile out to call Ellen before I could enquire for her.

"Sir! Any help" repeated the girl again.

"Ya I want to meet Ellen, she might have given you some note" I said in a very unsure way.

"Wait a second let me check" replied the desk girl.

While she started checking the register for the name: Ellen. I look into my mobile for Ellen's number and made a call to the number from where Ellen called me.

Ringing

With 2nd or 3rd ring Ellen picked up the phone.

"Hi, It's me Abhay here, I'm here at the hotel desk" I said and us relieved.

"Come to my room dear, its 249" Ellen said in an inviting way.

"Ok" I replied while disconnecting the line.

"Sir! Wait while I connect to Ellen" said the desk girl.

"She's staying at 249" I was confident this time.

The desk girl looked at my face while she turned few pages and there she got the name with the room number which I uttered just a few seconds ago.

Giving a pleasant smile, the girl showed me the way to Ellen's room.

"1 floor up and then to the right" said the girl.

"Do you need help? We can send our help boy with you to show you the room" continued the girl.

"No thanks I'll manage myself" I reply.

"Ok make the entry on the visitor's register?" girl points out the register and offered me a pen.

Taking the pen I filled up the required mentioned things and I started moving towards the room now. The feelings got harder with each step I took. Some inexplicable emotions were going through my mind. Counting every stair I felt like I am nearer to the destination. I turn right and there now I was standing outside Ellen's room.

I knocked at the door as I looked at my trousers and my shoes. Door was around by lovely lady smiling, wearing a black back less dress. She was a plump girl with blonde hair. Her curves were just visible by the dress she was wearing and I couldn't resist gazing at her.

"Come on in, I have to comb my hair then we'll go out for dinner" said the girl.

"Ya" I replied and by the time, my sweaty hands were showing that I was totally head over heals for her.

I entered the room and looked for a chair to sit while she went towards the dressing table to comb her hair. To start the conversation and to praise her beauty I encouraged myself to say something.

"Keep your hair as it is, do not knot them" said I.

"Ok honey" replied Ellen in a romantic way.

For her, these lines were casual but I needed time to be frank with her.

Boys can say any thing at back but ***jab samne kehna ho to unki bajj jaati hai.***

"Let's go to hotel's restaurant, I have heard it's one of the best in the country" said Ellen while putting her hand in my arm, just like we've known to each other for years.

This made me feel like her man and I felt confident now.

Being subtle now "Let's move lady" I said in a confident way.

And may be it was the thing lady, wanted to hear from me. We started moving towards the restaurant to eat something. Taking a side table for some privacy, Ellen took the menu card while I too looked at the menu card to look for the price list. Well in a student's life you always look for the price list first before you eat.

"How may I help you sir?" said the waiter in a very polite way.

"Mam would be pleased order" I rescued myself.

"Wine" said Ellen.

"Red wine then we'll decide the rest" continued Ellen.

Then the waiter came with the wine in a minute while I tried to settle myself.

Ellen filled the glasses and we started the conversation while taking sips of the red intoxicant. This was my first date with Ellen but it never seemed like we are meeting for the first time. We talked about everything from our professional life to the personal life.

Ellen then ordered some salad for dinner and I too joined her with the food. While taking food I found something moving between my thighs. It was Ellen's foot which were playing with my manhood and was massaging me between my thighs. I was intoxicated and so was she. It was not her fault but the red wine she had.

Look****eyes with a lusty look Ellen said "Come to my room I am waiting".

While I could think about what she's saying Ellen moved towards the door of the restaurant and went out and I kept looking at her buttocks which were moved as she moves towards the door. I too stood up on my feet but it was difficult for me. I was swinging still managed myself to be normal and started moving towards Ellen's room.

Drunken and out of my senses as I entered Ellen's room, my feet were unsteady. Her room was dim with the night lamp. I stepped into the room and I looked for Ellen. I could hear some sound of shower. I knew I was out of my senses, I took my second step with effort and started moving into the room. My gait was not normal now. I was swinging with the wine I just had. With a little more effort as I reached near the bed I fell onto the bed and I started taking heavy breaths. I knew I was out of senses.

Ellen came out of the washroom. She was only in towel. My eyes were closing but I could see her with my little opened eyes. I saw her wet hair and her smile which was more than inviting. I smiled back to her. It was an agreement that I had surrendered myself to her. She went near the mirror I gazed at her all the way praising her beauty and had a good look of her curves. I looked at her legs and I could see her skin and the shine of her body. I knew this was not the first time for her but for me I was like in heaven.

With my arms open I was on her bed begging her, to make love to me. Several thoughts came into my mind, my senses were not supporting me. I kept looking at her body while she kept combing her hair. With some strokes to her hair she looked into my eyes from the mirror image and her eyes whispered me to be calm and wait for sometime. I had almost lost my senses I was watching her my eyes closed.

As I felt some warmth on my chest I opened my eyes. As my eyes open all I could see was a beautiful lady onto me with her legs open crossed over my chest and her private parts near to my body. I could feel the warmth of her body and suddenly I saw my self with no shirt and she had already lifted her towel up to her hips. Her beautiful legs were folded and were near to my neck. I could smell her body and the beauties of her skin; I still wonder did when she managed to unbutton my shirt. She had something in her hand and her hair was covering her face. I wanted to see her face so I lifted my hand up and put my fingers in her hair and with my hand I held her hair, while I was doing this Ellen just peeped into my eyes and saw the lust I had for her.

By the time she had came to know that my tool had gone heavy and are ready to blow. Moving her buttock a little down she came on my tool to tease me more. She was on my hot rod and her whole body weight was giving me pleasure. I could feel she had gone wet down there and my hand fell on the bed, while her face got covered by her hair and I felt help less.

With her tiny eyes she gives me the "yes to make love now." But before I could start, Ellen gave her idea of this perfect love making.

"Let's start with your tattoo first and with my kisses and love I'll take your pain away" said Ellen while she stood up dropping her towel down on my bare chest. Her naked body was awesome to watch.

She went to her bag for her tattoo machine and with her machine she came on my body again.

"Lets make you more comfortable"; she said while unbuttoning my pants and putting her hand inside.

"We'll take care of it as soon as I'll have my name on your chest" said Ellen touching and feeling my urges for her.

Ellen again came into the position and her naked body was more nearer to me. My hand got life again while I was watching her making me slave for her lust. I started pampering her and cupping her curves. They were perfect to touch. While I was busy fondling her body, Ellen kept herself busy with tattoo machine. While arranging needle and putting ink cups on the bed Ellen started giving me instructions about the pain I'll go through while getting this tattoo on my chest.

All I could hear was that I am going to have tattoo of her name in Latin carved my chest at my heart's side. It was to be on left side so that she can be remembered always close to my heart and I should remember the one who took my virginity for the first time.

I could not say anything to my master, I was her slave. I had decided to have it first time with the girl whose had her name inscribed on my chest.

With the needle dribbling ink in my chest and paining all through my body, I could hardly care for anything now. My hands kept moving on her body feeling every cure of her. I pressed her booty to feel her buttock line which was going deep inside which I wanted to reach this time. But Ellen's hand kept moving for the tattoo and my hands to reach more of her.

Pain was getting more and more intense but whatever I was feeling down there was nothing as compared to it. I wanted it now no matter what happens next.

"Fuck me hard" I screamed aloud to get her attention.

"Wait honey for 5 minutes more" replied back Ellen smiling at my urge to get her.

The girl was enjoying the site, I was dying to have her once and to fulfill my needs. She has patience, she was not going to get distracted from it.

I lost my patience by the time now. As I was not getting anything, I wanted to go to pee, else my testicles were going to blow out my fluid. Yes I had some sperm ready to be flushed out now. My senses were not supporting me and finally my eye closed and I collapsed.

When I open my eyes everything was calm. My pants were off and Ellen was sleeping next to me. I wore my pants and I came out the bedroom area leaving my shirt over there. The liquor was out and all I had in my head was the little hangover. I was feeling pity for what I did. I went into the bathroom to look at my bare chest.

Tattoo was there, it was on my heart and it was something written in Latin may be her name or something.

I tried to remember what all happened between us. I went out of the room to get some fresh air while Ellen was there on the bed naked and her privates were all visible in the dim light but at the time I was not interested to look at her. I was feeling disgusted thinking about what I had been doing there and what ever I had gone through with the lady, when I had someone in my life whom I love so much then why I am ruining my life with such a bitch?

I went out bare chest as it was tough to wear shirt and I had scratches all over my chest. Her nails had also tattooed my chest.

I went towards the porch and looked at people moving here and there and suddenly I saw an angel looking at me. I still had my eyes on her and to my surprise she was Priya looking at me with her eyes full of tears talking to the desk girl while having the visitor's book in her hand. Before I could react to the situation Priya went out of the hotel with out looking back. I knew she had understood everything and there was nothing I could say now as I was the culprit.

———

I was not in intentions to do anything but I was caught in a wrong situation.

———@———

—19 Jan 3:00pm—
How I got caught

As I was continuously ignoring Priya for the past few days. She kept on trying my number and finally finding me no where in her life and in her contacts, Priya decided to call my friends. She called Ashit who lied to her saying he hadn't met me for past few days. Priya remained silent sad and lonely.

There was some one calling me all the time on my phone whom I kept on ignoring. He was Manav. Manav had a recent breakup with his Gf, which I didn't know and I thought Manav was calling me asking regarding Ellen and what all I am doing with her. So as to skip his dirty questions and his dirty mind I tried not to pick up his calls.

Finally adding more to my bad luck Manav decided to call Priya.

Both talked about their lives and to confirm about me Manav asked Priya where was and what I had been doing these days?

Priya in an unknowingly way, answered him that she didn't know where I was and she's trying to contact me. Manav unintentionally spoke out that I was in Delhi to which Priya gave a very surprised response.

Priya called each friend of mine she knew and asked for me but no one knew anything about me. Priya called my mom dad who confirmed her that I had gone to Delhi regarding admission but she knew it that I had lied to them and I am up to something which nobody knew.

Finally Priya called Varun who surrendered in front of her and told her that I was in Delhi for past few days but he didn't know where I was and what I was doing there but I was living with my friend over there.

Priya called Ashit and got the answer and finally Ashit told her everything still not telling the real truth to Priya. Priya asked my Delhi friend where she could find me, my friend gave her the whole information adding more to my misfortune.

My friend told her about the hotel I talked about once with him. Priya took her time and reached the hotel and to my bad luck the same time I came out of the room after the hangover and got caught in the porch shirtless.

——@——

After being caught

I went back into the room took my mobile out and tried Priya's number but her mobile was switched off.

I knew I couldn't do anything so I took a pen and wrote a note to Ellen and kept the note on her side leaving her there in the room and confessing my faults. I wore my shirt and went to my friend's place.

On the way I kept trying Priya's number to apologize to her and to tell her that I was guilty for what I did, and what she saw was the one side of the coin.

I was guilty so I didn't stay in Delhi and went back home the very day by night services.

The other side of the coin was: **my feelings for her were true but what happened to me that time I didn't know.**

12
Finally the Break up

Days were passing like I was in a hell. This guilt was killing me. I could face myself in the mirror because of this tattoo now.

It was there, my mistake had been imperiled on my skin .

I hadn't done anything with Ellen, it was just I was out of the way from my love life. Priya had to know that I was not involved with Ellen anymore.

My feelings for her were true and this love of mine, it was never fake for her.

I tried to call her a lot but Priya was not willing to listen to me.

A whole month passed this way, I had to do something desperately about it.

—1ˢᵗ **March**—

The weather was not in my favour. It started to rain and I knew Priya loved when it rained.

It was haunting me. I had to take my bold step now.

I messaged Priya.

"Listen to me please, talk to me or I'll do something crazy"

Still no reply came from other side.

I was all ship wrecked. I called Priya's little sis. Her number was busy

"Fuck" came from my mouth.

I got so hyper that I threw my phone at the wall. Every part of it broke open in front of me. I was so depressed by the act. Still thinking, Priya might connect me.

I fixed the phone right and put it on the table smoothly. I lay on bed thinking what if I would not have done this mistake in my life.

Priya always used to tell me that I'll go out of your life and then you'll repent.

All these thought were kaung me apart. I was abt to have a nervous breakdown. I could had have anything at that moment.

Ringing

Someone called me.

This shook my head

Priya's name came first in my head. But as I looked into the screen it was Priya's sis who was calling me.

"Hi Abhi bhaiya, you were calling me?" said Priya's sis.

"Ya but you were busy on the phone that time" I reply.

"Ya was talking to didi she didn't go to office today so she felt like talking to me, she was bit sad I think" said Priya's sis.

That's it, this much was enough for me to take any bold step.

"Ok will talk to you later" I end the call answering this much only.

I dial Vicky this time.

"Man I am going to Delhi I need to borrow some money from you" I say to Vicky.

"When are you going?" Vicky didn't know what I was going through but he was ready to help me without a question.

"Ok money will be in you account in an hour" replies Vicky.

I hang up the call and got a jacket onto me to protect my self from rain and a bag with few things I could find to help me out on the way.

I took first step out of my house, then a second thought came into my mind.

"I should try Priya's number once, before I go to Delhi?"

But my morals were high and I had already decided to go nothing could stop me.

I took my way out to the bus stop, waited for the bus to Delhi.

A million thoughts came into my mind, what to do??

I slipped my hand pocket andtook my mobile out to message Priya.

"I am coming to Delhi, meet me please. I want to meet you"

I had sent it to her.

It was enough from my part and I just started to wait for the reply.

She didn't reply.

Bus arrived, I got into the bus. Got a seat near the window and I started my journey.

Still Priya's thought were in my mind. I was in deep agony and the good weather was not making it pleasant.

Only thing I wanted, was to hear her voice.

I wanted to talk to her. I tried her number again but Priya didn't attend my call.

I knew she's not at office and was ignoring me.

I was in more guilt my girl was ignoring me.

I really wanted to say something.

I typed another message again

"I am in bus, started my journey I'll be there at Delhi after 4 hours."

She didn't reply either.

I tried to call her again, I was bit terrified thinking that Priya had finally made up her mind and had started hating me for my deeds.

I accepted I was wrong but my consicious had shown, me enlighten a second before something wrong happened and I really need a second chance for it.

I try her number again after it, I started calling her every minute.

Beep

Finally my phone beeped; it was Priya.

"I am getting irritated please stop this"

Finally whatever the message, Priya was replying atleast.

That was really enough for me.

I messaged her again.

"I am really coming, hope to get you as you know, I don't know much about the place and your address"

Nothing came from other side, I kept calling her but the difference was now that she was putting off my calls and it was making me happy that at least she was reading my messages.

It was raining heavily outside, bus had to stop for a while.

I didn't want anything else except her.

I was starved, so I took a cup of coffee before the bus started the journey again.

I could barely noticed that I had a Priya's message on my mobile

"Please don't come I won't meet you, go back home"

But nothing could have been done 2 hours journey had been covered and only 2 hours journey was left.

All this was tough I didn't know her new address and I knew nothing about Delhi, where did she live and what to be done?

I had decided to go to Delhi and rest was on God where he would take me and show me what to do.

I had decided in my mind that I won't go to my friend's place I'll sleep on the road but would definitely meet her, may be at her company's compound but I won't go back.

I tried to call her, this time to my surprise Priya's mobile was switched off. This was the most craziest part of the journey.

An hour's journey was left and I was about to reach Delhi and wasn't expected to happen.

I called her again, I wasn't right, still the phone was switched off.

No plan came into my mind, I knew only one person could help me, that was Priya's sis.

I called Priya's sis again.

Rings

"I am in Delhi and Priya's number is switched off, tell me what can I do now? I asked to Priya's sister.

"Bhaiya I don't know much about it but I can give you her room mate's number, she might help you out" replied Priya's sis.

It was enough for me.

"Message me I don't have any pen to write it down" I continue and put down the line.

Priya's sister got some clue that it must be a big fight that's why I am in Delhi to meet her.

With no time, message came with her friend's name and number.

The journey was about to end soon I had to take some action.

I decided to call her friend.

But my hands stopped as it was my last hope and I wanted to keep it for the last.

Finally it was time I reached Delhi.

Bus stopped at I.S.B.T terminal in Delhi, rest of the way I didn't know where to go.

Something had to be done from the point itself.

I tried Priya's number for the last time.

This time I was lucky, as Priya's mobile was switched on.

It runged but still no reply. It seemed like Priya was really uninterested to take my calls now.

She was really irritated by me.

But **where exists love nothing else matters**.

In a minute without, taking time, I typed message to Priya

"I am in Delhi, tell me where to go"?

Message came back" go to your friend's place or may be at your American friend's place!"

It was hurting and it was like as it she threw a stone on my face.

It pinched me so hard now I had decided to go on my own.

I remembered this much that Priya lived somewhere near by her old address and that was near Vasant Vihar.

So Vasant Vihar was my destination.

I had to take bus or an auto-rickshaw. I knew nothing about the place. I had always traveled to Priya and no where else in Delhi.

So for me Delhi was pure concrete jungle and I was lost.

I crossed the road from a crossing and went to other end. It rainly cats and dogs. I was all wet but my morals were high.

Now I had to take a bus to my destination. I asked a Papad-wala for directions.

It was my bad luck, that for my G.F's place I had to ask many strangers for the address, where as someone who knew me for past years was unwilling to help me, it was disappointing.

From the very day I learned that I like walking in the rain because no one ever knew my eyes were in tears with my heart thinking, my G.F didn't help and I took help of a stranger.

"Take bus from other side Babuji" said the papad-wala.

I cross the lane again.

I felt alone and I could easily hear each rain drop falling on the road.

"Take 621 number buses"

Thanking him I crossed the road and went back where, I started the my journey in Delhi.

I looked at every bus for its number then finally got a bus with number 621. I had to be brave enough I consoled and encouraged unfamiliar to me. I had to move ahead to get the destination – Priya.

Sitting in the bus.

I had followed a stranger's advice. Maybe I would have lost here in this big plastic city or maybe I would reach somewhere else but I had to meet Priya and that was final.

"Where you want to go?" asked the bus conductor from a seat, sitting next to door.

"Vasant vihar" I replied him like I knew the place where Priya lived.

I didn't want him to know that I didn't knew much about Delhi.

"20 rupees for it" conductor asked for the fare.

Handing him 20 rupees I wanted to know how long it would take to reach there, but my heart didn't allow me to do this.

Bus was all silent. Every one was enjoying the rain except me.

It was the summer rain but for me, it was like my heart was crying.

An hour passed by I was watched the whole scene even conductor didn't tell me that I had armed at my stop.

Finally I broke the silence I enquired the stranger near me "Sir I want to go to Vasant Vihar, is it near?"

"You are there my dear you asked right time, which lane?" asked the man sitting next to me.

I stood up and said "A"

"You are at B-sector better get off as soon as possible"

I knew I was making just a statement and this is like I had to reach that's it.

Now destination was near but where to go?

Finally after getting out of bus I slid my hand to reach the phone and decided to call Priya's friend.

Rings

"Hello" said Priya's friend.

"Hi" I reply.

"Who's this?" Priya's friend asks.

"You don't know me?" I said to skip the introductory part.

"I am Priya's boyfriend Abhi; she might have talked about me sometime" I continue and got over to the main topic.

"Yes I remember you, Priya was upset because of you"

"I am in Delhi" I said.

"Why" she replied back.

"I want to meet Priya can you help me please?"

"I can't help you much. Why did you travel so much?" she replied herself and telling me indirectly that she can't help me.

"I travelled for Priya I can't stand the pain I want to meet"

"Sorry where would you go?"

"I am at Vasant Vihar and I know, you people live here"

"Yes but we don't live exactly there. It is a bit far away"

"How much more than I have traveled till now, my love can't stop me tell Priya to meet me I am here till the night. May be she can make up her mind or you persuade her to meet me once"

"I can't help"

She disconnected.

I walked alone at Vasant Vihar

It was unfamiliar, I was at PVR Priya market.

I saw a board showing way to Vasant Vihar.

I knew nothing about the place all I know was I could go to Priya that's it

I was missing Priya more and more.

There were times we would meet each other there, but now time turned, she didn't even want to see me and left me alone in a big metro city.

But things were true, my deleverencies had made me realize and go through all me things.

I decided that what ever it takes I would convince to believe me that I really love her and I want her back in ,my life, what ever it may cost.

I took small steps and finally I reached PVR Priya's but I knew nothing what to do next.

I went inside alone.

I was missing Priya, it was raining again and I was all wet but I could not show my tears as we all know boys don't cry but who's going to notice that I am crying.

I need to cry and so I did.

Beeps

Message popped up. It was from Priya's friend

"She would meet you in half an hour at PVR Priya"

I typed back 'I am already at PVR Priya."

She didn't reply.

One thing was final that Priya was going to meet me, but what to explain was so difficult.

I was sad and had no words that could ever repair this relationship.

I had broken Priya's trust, may be my true love might get me near her. Nothing else could help I knew it well. Waiting for Priya, was the toughest job over I was starved for her. Yes I was just dying to hold her hand and say punish me anyway but not like this, I decided to ask her to slap me, scold me, do what ever she liked but to be with me. I kept waiting for hours I could not even message her. I knew I was wrong so I had to wait till my life takes me to her. Till then I would wait there. I would stay up for all night but would not go. Being deceive I stayed.

I kept waiting near the gate, sometimes I went inside, my legs were aching and I felt like blood draining from my legs but this couldn't stop me from meeting her.

From here I couldn't move back. Finally I saw my angel coming. I could not make an eye contact with her. I was guilty. She was with her room mate.

I knew I was wrong but I was here to make things right but the way she came, inside I knew deep that it would not work and nothing was going to happen. I still decided try to make things better.

I shook hand with her, but my body was numb I could hardly say any thing that time.

She started walking I could hardly move beside her side. I kept following her. Any relation was in a bad phase when two people who used to walk together, were walking away from each other. I kept following her, then it struck in my mind I should hug her and cry in front of her and confess for all my bad deeds and beg for a last chance. But my hands were so heavy at that time I could hardly move.

Priya took me inside the coffee shop where the I presented her me Anklet few months back.

I ruined everything, Priya's trust, my relation, everything. I was wrong and thus I was facing all this. These things kept revolving in my head.

We went upstairs, the hall was empty but we went upstairs, may be Priya had to scold me or so.

I kept following her silently. Finally she took the same seat where we met last time.

I also took the seat. It was all silent and no one was talking, Priya wasn't even looking at me. What to do in such case? I was like, melting on my seat. Where to start, it was like my tongue was buried in snow, I could not even feel it, then how talk about it.

"What would like to order sir?" said the boy.

Finally the silence broke.

"Lemon tea for two" I said.

"No I don't want anything" "Priya made her statement before the boy could place our order.

"Ok sir means 1 lemon tea" says boy.

"No I said two" I said with a heavy voice.

Priya didn't say anything this time but I knew she was not going to have it.

"I'll have two" I say to end this melodrama and to start talking.

Priya was still angry with me and it was clear from her face.

"How's you tattoo, is it still paining?" said Priya in a taunting way.

This hurt me most because I wanted to forget everything that happened that day but Priya was not willing to do so and now it was clear from her words that this was the end.

"Your drink sir" the boy placed the drink on the table.

I put double lemon in the drink to make it sourer and drank half of it.

It fired my empty stomach. I hadn't had anything since morning.

"What do you want from me Abhi"? said Priya in anger

"Don't you feel bad for ourselves and for what you did to this relation when it was going so smoothly" she continued.

"Why did you come here now?" she asked me.

"Sorry" I could only say this much.

"This is not about being sorry Abhi you broke my trust, you were with this girl and were in her room and you got caught, this time you are guilty. I wonder with how many girls you have slept with"!! Priya kept on pouring all her frustration on me.

Says what all I could hear because after some time I could only hear, buzzing sound in my ear and I felt I would collapse that time.

I added more lemon in my drink, I knew his time it would be unbearable for my stomach but I drank it in one sip. My eyes were burning after the drink.

I offered her the drink, but she refused.

"This is not a joke Abhi this is life and I am moving out of your life, hope one day you will understand what it felt like, when you hurt someone" Priya could only these words.

She was adamant on the decision and I knew it she would not change her mind for anything; I was wrong but I didn't play games with her but how to tell I went out of the room before anything could happen, it was her love which opened my eyes at the very moment. I could not do anything wrong and was not guilty. But saying such a thing at this time was all bullshit.

"I want a chance Priya" I said knowing this will never happen.

"Go to hell if you think this relationship will happen. It's a final **Break up**"!! shouted Priya.

"Break up" her words made an impression in my mind. Her voice got recorded in my ears and I could hear it again and again.

She looked in my eyes, this time I could not find any love for my self. I had hurt her more than I hurt myself this time. May be she had started hating me too and this was something I could not bear it.

I took the other glass of lemonade and gulped it. Priya knew it that I am hurting myself but she didn't care for this now. Things had changed for me.

"Let's go. There's nothing left for us to discuss, you shouldn't have come over here because things don't always work as you plan. Sometimes different things happen too" said Priya ending this date.

Bill came in a moment and I paid it off while Priya kept on looking outside the window. It was hurting me each second. I wanted things to settle down but how can I do all alone. This time I could not hold my tears. Priya moved out, I wiped my tears and pretended like nothing happened to me. I follow her again till we reach the gate, her friend was busy on the phone.

She didn't look back and they both said something and they went off.

It was not like she went but she had gone from this relationship, I was left alone. I could not take it.

I could not do anything, I stared at the road and the auto-rickshaw got smaller and smaller as it went away from me and finally I could not see it anymore. I started walking alone on the road I had no place to go now, I could call my friend and say that I am in Delhi and tell him to come and take me.

I stood at the road side time was killing me. I wanted this life to end three right at the very moment. I went to a near by shop, bought a cigarette and had a puff to relax.

Abhi will keep on loving Priya, was the last statement I had in my mind.

I will not lose her like this I was determined at last. I reached to the last puff of the cigarette and after some time my friend came and I went to his flat to rest after such a hectic day.

The very next day I went back home empty handed as I had been robbed of everything from me. My most precious gift, my Priya my only love.

Open window with a closed heart:

Open window with a closed heart,

I peeped out to get a start,

I can't see anything behind the hills,

Nothing in my mind not even ills,

May be a river or would grass,

But one day I'll go across.

I can see a house with a light,

Thing in the house seems to be clear and bright,

But in my heart its sill all dark,

May be in the relation I was monarch,

Either I was wrong or my dealings,

But one thing was sure I had some feelings...

Open window with a closed heart,

I may not be cute I may not be smart,

But I can feel the autumn coming by,

The happiness across the hills may turn into dry...

Sleeves are up now,

Face is down,

This broken relation is now my crown...

Cold winds were touching my face,

Just giving a shivering and her glace,

Breath feel heavy and cold,

Her words were harsh but were bold,

When she's was breaking I was looking in her eyes,

Her eyes were confident like her voice,

To live alone now was her final new advice.

I could not say anything I just stare

I knew one day with a heavy heart she'll come back here...

Should I accept her or should I not,

Is this relation broken or still knot,

Thinking of her may be making me her part,

Open window with a heavy heart,

Her words cannot keep us apart......

13
Making of the book

Broken into pieces I was all ship-wrecked and had no place to go. Life was nothing to me now. Priya and I had a break-up; I lived the worst nightmare.

I was a fault I accepted it and I had fought with my best friend too.

This was something I was never supposed to do. I knew I loved Priya so much that I couldn't live without her and I don't know what in this world I would do to make her feel I am not as bad as she thinks.

Nothing was there to rescue me out of my misery.

I tried to call Priya but she wasn't willing to pick up my calls and does not want to clear up the misconceptions. With each passing day I was dying with the thought of being an asshole on my part.

Being wrong was something which was more hurting & disappointed to me than her words during the breakup.

I knew if she would talk to me I would definitely convince her that I love her and had done nothing shameful to break this relationship of ours. Yes I was wrong at deliquencies that I didn't care for the relation but from my side I loved her. It was enough to cover up my mistakes and to forgive me.

—@—

—7ᵗʰ April—

It was Priya's B'day.

12 o'clock.

First time in my relation with her I had remembered her b'day and I wanted to call her first to make her feel special. I tried to call Priya.

Ringing

She didn't answer. Ringing goes on till it end up to the beep and simultaneously a tear rolled out from my eyes. I was wondering why I was crying? but then I found myself crying from the heart.

I knew I was repenting and was getting punished for whatever I had done.

But all I needed was a last try. I dialed her again this time her number was busy. I keep on trying her till I broke into pieces and decide to message her.

I was expecting to hear her voice after so long. May be she would be polite to me on her b'day but nothing happened as per my expectations.

I cried for some more time till I was exhausted then with my little heart I type the message.

"Happy B'day"

Nothing came from other side.

I knew this was going to happen but I was hurting my self trying to show her that I care.

Some wise words, when you love someone you can hope and you can expect, but you cannot expect them to love you back just the way you do.

I waited till 3' o'clock for any reply till my eyes closed and I felt asleep crying and kept staring at the mobile screen.

I was awaken the sound of crockery coming from the kitchen. It was late in the morning around 10 am. My eyes were aching and I was felt that I had a heavy hangover. Taking two **Disprins** from my cupboard I came back to my senses. I forgot everything that had happened last night.

I searched for my phone.

It was not at its place for charging. I went ready to the bedroom get tea from the kitchen.

Then suddenly Priya's thought came to my mind.

Today is Priya's b'day and I had messaged her at night.

I search for the mobile all over in my room. It was buried under my bed sheets.

I took it out and looked for any message.

I had message from someone.

Wishing to God before I opened the message I pressed the show button.

Yes it was Priya's message.

"Take care"

I read this much message and I fell into my bed. I was still hoping to get a good answer from her side. I knew it was impossible but I was still dreaming to get everything right.

For me to read the whole message was something impossible. I put the mobile down and went into the washroom.

Taking a shower I cried and thinking what next she would have messaged me I finally deicided to make the heavy move to read it.

Finally out of the room I took the mobile again in my hands, the massage was still opened.

"Take care Abhi I will not come back, don't show any care to me"

I read the whole message. I felt like a thunder just struck me. Coming back into my senses I closed the message. This was something I was not expecting.

I wanted to message her again now but what to do. I felt restless. Finally I decide not to do so.

I want her b'day to be celebrated the same way as we did, when we were together.

I wanted to give her flowers. But I did not have her address. I decide to call Priya's friend to get her address.

Ringing

"Hello" I said as soon as her friend picks up the call.

"Hello who's this" said Priya's friend.

"It's me Abhi" I reply back.

'Who Abhi" said the girl.

"Oh! Ya Abhi I remember you Priya's friend" she continues as soon as she remembers my name.

"Ya Abhi, yaar can you help get Priya's address" I asked her, keeping my fingers crossed.

"Sorry, Priya has told me not to give her address to anyone and especially you" said Priya's friend in a harsh tone.

"Sorry I want to help you but I can't" she apologized too.

But the thing was it was not her but Priya who did not want to give me her address so this girl didn't have any fault.

"Thanks anyways" I put down the line. I did not give up.

I thought to get keep from her sister as she had helped me a lot through all these bad phases.

With no time I called her sister.

Ringing

"Hello Abhi bhaiya" said Priya's sis as my number was known to her by now.

"Ya it is me Abhi" I said in a sad tone.

"Can I have Priya's address" I said but I knew the answer would be same.

"Sorry bhaiya Priya has told..." I put down the line as I heard the same statement again.

I knew this was going to happen but still I was trying and this time it didn't hurt me anymore.

I went out of my house to take some puffs. Lighting the cigarette I looked into the card gallery. My legs took me there for something I wasn't planning.

While my cigarette was in my hand I picked up one card which took my attention.

It was a sorry card and a b'day card for lovers.

I bought the card knowing I couldn't give it to her but I knew it was going to happen some day.

I took 21 roses bouquet too for her and finally came back to my room.

I keep the card and bouquet in my cupboard and lay down on the bed.

Finally the day passed by, calling up Priya and she ignored all my calls.

I wanted to talk to her on this very special day but nothing happened as per I decided.

I took a notebook and wrote something that I wanted to express. With tears fallingon the notebook and the pen moving fast as I wrote everything I could write to her.

This made me feel relaxed and I wrote for the whole week. I felt like talking to Priya as I wrote my feelings on the book.

Finally I decided to confess everything and every incident from the very university incident and Sana incident like a confession in the notebook.

Things got accumulated and finally the day came when I wanted to give all the stuff to Priya.

While busy with the notebook I called Priya a number of time but she kept ignoring me and with some messages I managed to get back Priya's trust to meet me once again.

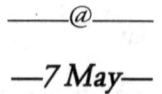

—7 May—

Finally the day came when me and Priya decided to meet for a last time. I took everything from the bouquet to all cards I had bought for her and went to Delhi again.

Time passed so quickly this time as I was eager to meet her.

This time I decided to meet her at PVR Priya market. I knew nothing would work out but all I had was to confess and I needed some nice place for it. I needed some place comfortable, so the idea to meet at PVR Priya was exactly what I wanted. This time I was the one to arrive first at the decided place. I knew I had this last chance to get myself out of this guilt and I could do anything for this. Priya took her time and she came alone this time without her friends. Things were going my way so far.

As I was waited for her at the side of the gate, Priya entered but she did not see me. I was hiding behind the hoardings.

Priya started walking inside the market and her eyes were searching for me. She took her mobile out of the pocket and dialled. I kept following her as I could not say anything in the phone.

"Hey Priya"; said I a bit aloud from behind.

Priya looked behind, as she knew it was me calling.

"Oh hi" said Priya in a way as if she felt pity on me.

I felt very bad but controlling my anger I gave a smile to her as if nothing has happened. I knew I was fooling my self. I just had to be a little bit fake so that I could make her listen to me and I wanted to give her some stuff I had with me all these days.

This stuff in my room was killing me from past these months and I had cried a lot looking at them. Now it was time for this stuff to return to their original owner.

We had dinner together. The weather was cool and romantic. It was just perfect for a romantic couple and I was crying inside while thinking, why I was alone in such a lovely weather. As we finished our dinner now it was time for us to depart anyhow. Priya knew I had something to give to her and moreover I also knew it was time to confess but I was in a dilema tensed.

To make a start and to get out of the market I asked Priya to take road just across it.

I had to make some bold moves I was preparing for it so that I could look in to her eyes without any distraction. While I confess what I had in my mind.

Priya and I started taking a walk with the things still in my bag.

Walking around 3 minutes in silence, I knew I had to make a start now else she'll move back and I'll miss the last chance of mine.

To make a start I said,

"As we lived a life together and I had talked so much with you on some good topics and under bad conditions"

"There were some bad times we faced and some good times together but this thing never happened that we stopped talking and you had such a bad impression of mine in your mind." I continue while Priya kept at looking to the cars and the busses passing by.

It seemed like she was uninterested to listen to my confession but still nodded her head once to show that she was attentive to what I said.

I didn't bother this time I wanted to continue so that I could not break before the confession ended.

"Priya this time I really wanted to confess to you and I could have made it on the phone but I wanted you to see loyalty in my eyes as I confess to you and still if you find me wrong I would call my self a loser" I started making the confession.

These words of mine took her attention. Priya stopped walking and we stood under a tree there.

I looked into her eyes and I could see her shimmering eyes peeping into mine saying that I have hurt her and I am doing all this just to show that I care.

But deep in my heart I was crying. I had to take a step but my knees were cold and I could not say anything as I wished to kneel down before I could confess the rest.

I stared into her eyes and started confessing the rest.

"Priya I really want to say I am sorry for what ever I did and I am really sorry I hurted you unintentionally, if you love me just give me a chance and I promise I'll not repeat it again in my life, please honey I am loyal and my heart is just pious as I it is so because it still loves you."

Saying this I did not realize when I had bent on my knees and held her hand.

I kept looking at her and she also kept looking into my eyes no one was saying anything at the moment. It was like our eyes were saying something to each other.

Our eye contact was talking, asking for forgiveness and Priya looking into her heart what to do whether to forgive me or not.

But the bloody phone rang and distracted the whole bond. If the thing had continued a minute or two I could have Priya back.

She took her mobile and started to walk back but she could not speak anything to the caller. I followed her till I reached the gate and all the emotion Priya had for me ended, so ended my last chance.

"Shall we depart" Priya said in a painful manner.

I could not speak anything and took the cards out and handed over to her.

Looking at the card, Priya took an auto-rickshaw and went back to her place without warning a good bye or giving any second look to me.

I went back inside the market and took out my last cigarette, lit it up and took a puff out of it.

While doing it I kept thinking about what could have been done if I had continued the talk. Priya might have come back if I had made some more bold steps and would have said I Love her more than anything. Thinking about it I end my cigarette and went back to the gate. My mobile was showing low battery sign and I had to reach I.S.B.T. as soon as possible now so as to catch the last bus.

I knew Priya might melt after reading my cards but this was not just to show off. It was something I had for her in real.

I had loved the girl more than anything so I was in pain.

Time grew so quickly now and I finally took the bus to my home disheartened.

On my way I felt something was left in my bag. I look into it; it was something I had written for her all the way.

Yes the notebook of my feelings I had for her was left with me. I took my mobile out to convey her but nothing seemed right anymore. My mobile was off due to low battery and I was ruined now.

I felt restless and put down my head.

Finally I decided what has to be done will be done tomorrow and none I should try to sleep.

Very next day I reach home in the morning the first thing I do is to charge my mobile.

While charging I tried Priya's number but it was switched off. Something bad had happened. May be Priya had called me at night and she might had thought that I had gone forever and had switched off my mobile she had finally made her decision to end up the relation finally and ending my hopes for her.

Till evening I tried to call her but nothing much happened, it remained silent.

I tried her friend's numbers too, but she also turned me a cold shoulder same as her sis who said "end the crap bhaiya, she'll never come back now"

—@—

—15 June—

Days passed like hell, I was all alone half word found with my diary I was writing thinking as if I was talking to Priya.

I tried everything so that I could reach Priya but no one helped me out, not even my friends.

Every body knew I was at fault so no one came of my rescue. I was left alone and it was right on their part because I had hurt a loving heart.

I wrote everything from my very first mistake to my very first moment of joy.

Finally the scene broke as Aman came to my house searching for some books. He looked into my notebook and without permission read a chapter of it.

Aman was my junior but was like my best friend.

"Sir why don't you get it in a manuscript, type it out and get it published"? said Aman.

"No dear it is something for Priya and it will reach her one day".

"No you should try it once, I know some good publisher who can help you out" replied Aman giving me a life time opportunity.

"Ok we'll think over it" replied to Aman ending the topic.

Finally after Aman left my place but had given me something to think.

This was God's grace or what but there was something Aman had said to me which kept on ringing in my mind.

Time passed Aman kept on asking me was gonna do what the script.

I tried to ignore it till, I finally decided to make it a manuscript and get it published.

I looked for the format over internet for the book and this was the first time I was using my computer for something good.

Finally after a month the book was ready to be taken to the publisher.

I finally called Aman the very day it finished.

Ringing

"Hey Aman can you help me with the publisher I just finished my book" I said in joy.

It was something to cherish after so long and especially after a break up.

I still cried for Priya all these days while writing to her and calling her every day thinking the phone might be working.

"My uncle is a publisher I'll give you his email id just mail it to him and wait for the response." replied Aman.

Taking Aman's email id I continue with my work and life and finally forgot about the book. All I could remember was Priya and her memories now.

MY LAST POEM

As I lay down on the bed
On my pillow I lay my head
Watchn' my room all dark and damp
Try to see you but I can't

I try to close my eyes and try to sleep
But your care didn't let me dream
I feel like I've been torn apart
Am broken as it seems
As I am not a liar and not that smart
And that's why I am helpless my part

I turn side to side, I feel so restless
And I know today am not gonna sleep
I know that am gonna still misis' you
It is something I always do
There was a time when you call me as we
Do you think still just like me?

I can hear the clock ticking so slow
Then why our luv went by so fast

Just when I went wrong in a luvn heart

And you make this luv not happen so last

Is this how you feelings change and lost?

I could not sleep and I couldn't not dream

As I get up in the morning still all same

You may be your best but and still in pain

My daily routine quickly takes

It seems you're not luvn me coz it's all my mistakes...

Feel like going back to the bed to stay sometime there

Your distance is what I can't bear

You said you'd never leave me and you care

Then where are you when I want you here

My daily routine went so same nothing good and nothing new

I am hurting myself all by thinking of you...

Some how I get on the road and to street I board

Going down to your street

With your thought in my mind

And a heart which skips a beat

Streets are crowded and my mind too

There's nothing now I can't do for you

You never seem to wave me good bye

It was always last we met and you just make me cry

As I pass thru your house

Just to the right

I speed up a bit to skip this sight

I see your close window and the door

I know no one will be there waiting for me any more

The road here seems to be so long

What on the earth should do right to end this wrong

I can imagine a girl there with a tear

With this thought on my side

Are these things you still hide?

Suddenly all thoughts disappears and go

I turn my face and ask why

It feels like my heart will go cry

I say sorry in my heart and passes by
All I can do now is to try

You just said you will never see my face
And now you are happy at your place...

"I was your bf
I've been torn apart
I know now you had left me and this thought
And that have broken me apart"

And that day a Abhi died again
Writing this poem all in tears and pain:

Poem is:

You'll be broken into tears
As you'll read my death letter
I know you don't fell any good for me
But as I am gone, now from inside it
Will make you feel better.

I'll be gone and I'll never return

This thought will be end up with my burn
I'll send you my last letter and a picture
With a quotation written on its back
"To my gf" and all the stuff packed

You gave me emotions and took my life
I wished I could see you and look into your eyes
If id never hurted you would be so wise!

I had never forgot you and this you know
I'll never change I'll show
If things would have changed'
I'll never let you go

Always urs Abhi

And a Abhi died again
Left by Priya all in pain
I am now said "I" only
Coz you've left this relation
And set yourself free!!!

14

The reconcile

—*10 July*—

The e-mail came with a good response from the editorial review of my writing.

I did not bother to share anything with anyone. I was drowned into the sea of tears and pain which was my breakup gift from my sweet little GF.

Now liquor was my only friend.

I was asked for the bio-sketch with a synopsis of my book.

I started writing while I was drunk and mailed the publishing house. I started waiting for any further queries. Days passed and the thoughts of the book faded. But I did not share this news with anyone not even with my mom and dad. I wanted to let Priya know first about it that I've something which everyone is going to read.

I took my mobile and dialled Priya's number with a very numb heart, to my surprise Priya had changed her number as she doesn't want any contact with me.

I was soaked into blood tears now.

—@—

—*1ˢᵗ Aug*—

It was a day to celebrate; finally I was recognized as a writer by my publication house. I was asked to meet them for my book and its covers at

Delhi. This was the happiest day of my life since Priya had left me.

I wanted to share my happiness with her but I had no connection with her now. So I remained silent and went to Delhi alone to meet my publisher to finalize my book, to meet for the copyrights and the royalty signup.

After meeting with the publisher and deciding everything, I came back.

—@—

—*10Sep*—

Finally my book was on shelves, Priya was still missing from my life.

My first copy was in my hand and was packed up for Priya. I had to find her and hand it to her; it was decided from the very first day. I call up all my friends to celebrate at PVR Priya market at the very place of the breakup. This place had become very close to my heart.

It was time to celebrate my book which was on stand. I called Priya up for the last time but nothing happened as I had thought.

It was party and every one was present. To my surprise came a lovely lady with a rose bouquet and a lovely smile on her face.

It was Priya, it was from the past 6 months I had not seen her and hadn't seen such a lovely smile that could take my breath away.

I was shocked how she came to my party. Priya stood at the entrance searching for me. She was looking like an angel just the way I wanted, in a white kurta and blue jeans. I stared at her for a while and then suddenly started moving towards her to greet. Priya smiled at me which seemed to be like she had forgotten everything that had happened in the past.

"Hello" I greeted Priya but my voice seemed to be low and with the happiness my eyes were crying.

"Congrats" said Priya handing her sweet bouquet.

Taking the bouquet in my hand I looked at Priya. She was looking as pretty as ever.

I felt like crying and melting in to her arms and begging for the last chance so that I can be with her. But I knew nothing is going to happen and at the moment she has visited me like a guest so I decided not to do any melodrama.

"Abhi why are you crying"? replied Priya with tears in her eyes.

"Am" It tried to hide my tears as I wiped off my tears from my face quickly.

"Let's move outside and talk" Priya tried to keep me off the embarrassment.

I went out with Priya.

"Let's walk a while" said Priya.

I could not say anything except following her steps and looking at her feet moving.

——Leaving the party——

To make a start while going out of the market Priya said "lets have a walk to the road side."

I kept following her without anything in my mind. It was all blank. I kept thinking Priya might have something to say but I was hopeless.

Priya and I started talking a walk and she had a gift still in her hand. It was a gift wrapped.

Walking for around 3 minute silently she stopped under the tree without saying anything.

To make a start she says:

"As we lived a life together and we had talked so much with each

other on some good topics and bad conditions"

These lines were sounding similar to me so I paid a little more attention to that she intended to say, I keep my head down like a culprit listening to her words.

"There were some bad times we faced and some good times but this thing never happened that we stopped talking and you had such a bad impression of yourself on your mind." Priya continued kept on saying these lines. I could hear the sounds of the cars and the busses passing by.

It seemed like she wanted to make some last note, still I nodded my head to her showing I was attentive to what she wanted to say.

"Idiot can't you look into my eyes when I confess something. You always make me cry with your words and when I want you to see my loyalty in my eyes you are not interested"

Priya said all this in a single breath.

"This time I really wanted to tell you that I could not understand you and your love for me but as I look for you now. I don't find you any wrong and if you will not come back to me now I'll call my self a loser" she started making her words like she still thinks me as her BF.

These words of her took my attention. My eyes were still wet and I wish this time that it should rain so that I can hide my tears. I look into her eyes and I could see her shimmering eyes peeping into mine saying "*c'mon make a move, hold me in your arms*".

But deep in my heart I was crying I had to take a step but my arms were cold and I could not bend them as I wished to hold her tight and just hug her for the rest of my life.

I stared into her eyes and started saying words I had in my heart for the past six months:

"I have two news for you'

One is good and other bad

Good thing is I am with you! and bad news is how to be with you."?

Saying this I could not speak anything and Priya knew these words are mine. It is my guilt. So to give me a chance Priya stopped me by saying "*If I am not with you I think I'll get lost in this big world. It's a big large world for people like us. And living a moment without you is missing a lifetime.*"

She started crying like a baby and just hugged me tightly.

I too hugged her and to make her feel better I whispered in her ears "*The moment that can change everything. I don't know what is happening to us and between us. But when I am with you I feel like home. I promise to be faithful to you for the rest of my life.*"

Then Priya handed me the gift she had for me.

"Open it Abhi" said Priya handing me the gift.

With no time I open the wrapper and find my book. Yes, Priya had read it and this was what I wanted in this life time.

"Hun' I read it the very moment I found it on the shelf. And found that the pain you went through.

I always thought this was your time to do the sacrifice as I always did but I never saw the other side of the coin. But since I have seen the other side of the coin I can't stop myself from loving you." Priya continued.

"But I still want the original book of yours, I mean all those pages you have written for me, they belong to me" Priya says with a big smile on her face.

All I could do here was to nod my head with a smile.

"Love you always" says Priya and there goes the exchange of kiss. I held my girl tight and found love again.

Some wise words: You know what, no matter what you do, if you have a true love in your life who also loves you that much ... you are there with it always.

———@———

"LOVE NEVER FADES..."

Story ends but the Love never ends....

Note from the Author

How the book began:

I was writing the for the past few years but I never noticed, it started with few lines for my girl friend which finally turned into chapter and as pages piled up more and more... it took the shape of a book.

Most of the incident in the book are not true but the healthy feeling which I went through with my love life helped me to express my feelings and love, which was penned down in the book. I never had an idea to get it published but as I got screwed, went through my break up phase, this book helped me to get over the melodrama. I want to thank my lil' sweet gf for giving me feelings when she entered my life, helped with the love story and then finally by her silent breakup for pity which gave me the courage to speak out in the world, look into the eyes of critics, to face rejections ...

Thanks to all who discouraged me with their words, all the way strengthening me and my thoughts to go with my book further...

From the real Priya:

From the first Reader:

I wish for the author of this book who is my roommate and a good friend of mine to achieve success for his book.

May God bless him with more pains, so that more emotions can be penned down. I would like to thank him to indulge me with the exercise of reading his book and give me immense privilege to be his first reader and asks me for further suggestions and reviews.

After reading his book, which was the first novel of mine as a reader as I had no interests in reading novels, I thank him for making me curious to read more such books in the near future.

"May God bless him with what he desire."

Dr. Aman Monga, M.P.T. (Ortho.), MMU.

From the Author's Family:

Growing up in a closed atmosphere in a valley of J and K we never knew Nikhil will take such initiatives in his life like this. He many a times mentioned about the book and his writing but we never knew he's so much serious about the book and all the stuff.

But the very day he came up with the e-mail saying he's in contact with publishing house for the publishing work for his first book, we came to know about his serious writing skills.

"Our best wishes are with him always."

From brothers, sisters and all members of the Mahajans Family.